CHANCE ENCOUNTER
❦ BOOK ONE ❦

A PRIDE & PREJUDICE RE-IMAGINING

NEY MITCH

Reader, thank you so much for once more giving a new read a try. I confess that this is the first time that I've written a new Jane Austen reimagining in a while. Therefore, both you and I are taking chances here. Let's see how we do.

With Jane Austen, she still captures my imagination. If you have given me a chance again, I'm assuming she has captured yours. We all wish that she had lived longer, for if she had done so, she would have been able to write more novels or finish ones that she had already begun. We wish that *Sanditon* was completed. Some of us also desire that she had decided to finish *The Watsons* rather than casting it aside. We hope, and we dream, but it is not so.

Therefore, we travel onward, taking her characters as far as they *will* go and *can* go. Yet, every now and again, we look back and hope that Miss Austen understands why we cannot forget her characters, but rather we keep bringing them back to life so that they remain beside us… always keeping us company in a way that only they could.

Readers, thanks again for coming back, and always, this tale is dedicated to you!

Also, I would like to give a special thanks to my publisher, editors, cover artist, and Helen Roberts-Vickers for all their incredible work and consideration. You all are brilliant!

Ney Mitch

CHAPTER 1

FEAR UNDONE

I talk of dreams.

I speak of desires.

For in the world we live in, we humans rarely do anything else but those two things. Within the very secrets of our hidden souls, we are fed by both those objects. Dreams belong in the domain of the mind while desires lie expressly in the province of the heart. We know that they feed us.

However, outward we present a whole other portrait. We paint ourselves differently when in society. For no matter how we feel within, from without, in the very eyes of the world, we must always put on a proper face. We must be expected to always appear as almost idle, lacking occupation…and we must not present ourselves as one who is ever dreaming and desiring anything.

Yet, both those items are never farther from our thoughts.

Charlotte Lucas, one of my dearest friends, secretly is feeding on both of those internal sources at present. I may not be near her, yet I know that she is. The letter she had sent me is now resting on my desk in my room, and though her words are sanguine, I know better.

I know the truth.

For, though there be a part of Charlotte that I do not know, there is still the part that is familiar to me.

I know, now more than ever, that she wishes so much had not occurred as it had.

Looking down at the letter, I can imagine her expressions and countenance as she wrote it. She would not be weeping as she composed this missive, and that much was apparent for the lack of tear stains that were on the page. Yet, she would have been frozen over from the situation…of things in her life not going as planned.

Packing a black dress in my wardrobe chest, as well as other items, I recalled the words in the letter almost accurately…

My dearest Lizzy,

I write to inform you of news which you have perhaps already heard. No doubt, with the comfort and connections between Lucas Lodge and Longbourn, my father, mother or siblings may have already delivered this message.

My late husband, my poor Mr. Collins, has recently passed away, and thus I have been, at so young a time, been placed into the role of widow. My father is to come up to Hunsford parsonage so that I am able to assemble all my belongings. In a month's time, I shall have to quit Hunsford entirely, to make way for the new Reverend who is to take my husband's place.

If you so desire it, I wished for you to accompany him and my sister to Hunsford, while I prepare myself for this new step in my life…the step for which I am to return back to my father's home, where I shall once more be a burden.

Lizzy, if you do not desire to come, then do not. Yet, since both you and I have experienced a recent tragedy in our family, and our fates have often been inextricably bound, then I would love for you to assist me when I am in this frightful hour.

I am yours, etc.
Charlotte

Charlotte Lucas, who had very briefly been named Charlotte Collins from marriage, was now to return to the life she once had. She was a widow, yes, but when had those ever been of any great power in our world?

Never!

Therefore, she was as the rest of us were: of little importance, and indirect as to her future. Like us Bennet sisters, she was a leaf along the wind of the plans of fate.

———

When done packing my things, I went downstairs to my father's study. When reaching the door, I placed my hand on the doorknob but stopped there.

My actions were as they always had been when going to see my father. However, my action from without would be completely different from the lack of action of the figure who would have been within.

As was my way, I was undergoing old motions—the same feelings of revisiting a place where you would often glimpse a loved one whom you had recently lost.

On the other side of that door, father often sat there reading his book—as well as trying his very best to escape the constant sound that my mother and sisters made just by speaking. And, if I imagined it, he would still be there, sitting with a book in his hand, with a twinkle in his eye that hinted at his sardonic wit.

And then I would open the door, and it would be as it always was, every day, for the past four weeks.

I opened the door…and my father was not there.

After all, he hadn't stepped into that room for two fortnights—ever since he walked out of it, making his way to the front yard, where a sudden seizure struck him, and he fell down where his eyes closed forever.

I remember that moment to this very day, for it was I who had seen him from across the gardens. Jane and I had glimpsed his collapsing form, and with quick dexterity, we raced towards him, with me reaching him first. I rolled him over, to make him lie on his back, and in his eyes was a terror, a horror and fright.

In my arms, my father had passed away, filled with a dreadful thought, and disturbed expression, and the loss of clinging to life for as long as he could before his heart beat its last.

When Jane reached us, his eyes lost their life, his last breath escaped him, and I let my head collapse on his chest.

After we buried him, I wondered what it was like when he took that last walk from his study to the yard. Did he feel a sensation of mortality clinging to his consciousness? Did he take that last walk from his study because he felt death lashing out at his heels, and therefore, with a burst of life, he dashed out to the gardens to see the sun for the last time? Like a drowning man who is trying to reach the surface of water.

Or did he feel the pains in his chest and raced out, trying to find Jane or me? Was he rushing out to see us, to use us as his last grasp at life?

"Elizabeth…" he had gasped before his eyes had completely lost the light that was in them. My name was the last name that he had spoken before he died.

A memory such as that could continue to haunt a person.

"Father?" I whispered to his study, despite knowing there would be no reply. "Father?"

When no sound came back to me, I collapsed in his chair, and my whole body began to shake.

My father was gone. Mr. Bennet, the master of Longbourn, was gone forever.

And therein departed my beloved parent and one of my sole defenders in this world. For, when mother and father argued about the eternal question that was *me*, my father always had an answer, and that was what helped me survive in this world. A constant stream of defense flowed from him. Now that he was gone, that stream would dry up and had no more source, and the chief consolation of my life, of my will and strength, always being given nourishment would wither and break.

By god, how had it come to this?

———

Knock! Knock! Knock!

I wiped my eyes, but it wasn't soon enough. My eldest sister Jane entered, and she saw my crestfallen countenance.

"I had a feeling that I would find you in here," Jane observed, "looking to commune with our father's spirit?"

"Looking to channel our father's mind," I retorted, forcing a smile, "with a wit such as his, I refuse to allow it to die. If I did, I do not think that he would look on me kindly for that."

"At least know that he is looking on you always," Jane responded. Our father was a man who could sit in a room and let his imagination take him anywhere and elsewhere, but I never thought he let his imagination stretch so far that he would have left us fully behind. Therefore, I think he sees you out of the corner of his eye."

"If that be so, then we shall forever be a glint—and a glint is more than a spec, and a spec is more than a bit of air. I'd hate to think that our memory got that light and could be carried off by the mere bit of wind that blew around him." I leaned back in his chair. "I know it, but I can't believe it. He is gone. He is really gone."

Jane sat down beside me on our father's footstool.

"Yes, he is," Jane responded. "I miss him."

"And the rise and fall of a month is not enough time for us to move past that stage of grieving. Therefore, I think we have the right to let our pain remain in the proper place."

"Jane!" Our mother cried, "And Lizzy! Lizzy! And Jane!"

Our eyes closed when we heard our mother, Mrs. Bennet, call for us.

"We could pretend that we do not hear her," I offered.

"Lizzy, you know that is not the proper way of being," Jane responded.

"We have three younger sisters, let her call them," I said, standing up. "They are one more in number than us, therefore, they would do the job most credibly at being our substitute."

"Perhaps she has something special to say to us."

"Or more of her tales of woe of now being a widow."

We walked upstairs to our mother's bedroom, prepared for the scene of a grieving widow who had all her nerves attacked by panic and fear of being no longer able to both equally love and vex her husband.

After all, that's what husbands could be good for: to love one minute and be at odds with in the next.

My father was gone, and thus, my mother lost a husband and one of her chief opponents when it came to her domestic decisions. How could she cope without her deceased love and constant antagonist?

When entering our mother's room, Jane and I saw the immediate reason for why she only called for us; two of our three sisters, Mary and Kitty, were already present. Lydia was away, visiting a friend.

And seated in the chair by the window, wearing the black that comes from being a woman in mourning, our mother sat, fidgety, hysterical and constantly dabbing her eyes with a handkerchief— even though she was not crying. If I did not feel sad as well, I would think it was a comedic sight.

"Oh, there you are!" she gasped. "Have you both laid fresh flowers on your father's grave, for you know that it is quite your turn today?"

"We have not yet done so," Jane responded, "for we were just about to go and pick from the flowers now."

"Do so immediately!" she cried. "Or be forever labeled as ungrateful girls."

We did not reply to this shocking outburst because we knew the source that it stemmed from; our mother's nerves had increased ever since father passed away. Ergo, the tragedy of his loss, mingled with her naturally high-strung disposition, made her even more subject to sudden outbursts that could be directed towards anyone, even Jane.

"And Jane," our mother continued, "have you finally been able to convince your stubborn sister here to give up this scheme to visit Charlotte Collins yet?"

"No, mama," Jane answered, secretly flustered, "for there have been a great many things to do today, and it quite escaped my mind."

"How can you forget!"

"Oh, ma," Kitty wailed, "Lizzy is here, so why do you not tell her yourself?"

"Aye, mama," I concurred, "for I think I can receive whatever you have to say… if something else still remains to be said about something."

"Stop sounding like your father."

"I was wondering if you had noticed." Soon after I said this, I stifled my smile. After all, now was not the time to be smiling. My mother noticed this.

"Cold-hearted child, to be smiling a month after your father passed away. Have you no proper feeling?"

"My feelings, I believe, rest in their proper place. I smile for father because I know that he would not want me to forget that practice. It was eternal frowning that he found to be distasteful. But as for lightness of expression, well… I believe that he often tolerated that with equanimity."

"Mother," Kitty interrupted, "Lizzy does have a point. I am certain that she misses father, but I doubt that he would want her to regress into a creature of coldness."

"Precisely," I agreed.

"Enough of this talk," our mother declared, "and very well, I shall undertake to persuade you myself. Elizabeth, I forbid you to go to Hunsford Parsonage to see Charlotte Collins."

Ah! At last, the piper popped.

"You distract me from my point," she snapped, "and I will be heard. Lizzy, you owe nothing to Charlotte. And I think that it is most high-handed that she even requested for you to visit her at this time. What with your father not being cold in his grave."

"Mother," Jane began, now sitting in a corner while reading a book. "Though our father's passing has indeed put our family in distress, it is not wise for us to advise Lizzy not to go to Charlotte at this time. For her loss must equal our own."

"And pray, she deserves it!" Our mother cried. "To have married Mr. Collins, with the express desire to disoblige our family, only for Mr. Collins to die so soon into their marriage—that is what I call judgment doing its work properly."

"While I am quite certain that Fate worked its very best to conspire alongside you in giving Charlotte her just comeuppance," I retorted, "we must work our best not to do anything that would make Judgment wish to turn her frightening eye upon us." I saw father's armchair and decided to sit down in it. "After all, Fate does not owe much loyalty to anyone. Therefore, if my departure to visit Charlotte seems to be more than her due, then think of it this way, it is me sending our good intentions to appease the very muse that we were just speaking of…especially since there is a part of the situation that neither of us know of."

"And what would that be?" Kitty asked, who had recently just re-entered, with some material and a bonnet preparing to work on it.

"That Charlotte may be with child," I said, with such firm simplicity, that it had a magical sort of grand effect on the room. After my answer was given, my mother and my sisters, Jane, Mary and Kitty, stopped what they were doing and turned to me.

"And if she is with child," I continued, "there is the chance that the child may be born a boy."

"And if so," Mary said, looking up from her book and turning to us, "then we shall start this way all over again."

"Yes, we shall," I concluded. "Our father has passed away, and Mr. Collins passed away soon after. We were able to have the tragedy from another corner elude us, but perhaps that elusion was only a temporary one. If Charlotte is with child, then we have to settle the possibility between us that she could deliver a boy, and that child shall be the heir of Longbourn."

"And if that would be the situation," Jane voiced, her tone serene, but hiding the worry that lay underneath, "then we have only less than a year before we can be removed from Longbourn and then forced to make our way in the world."

"Lost among the winds of confusion," Mary sighed.

"If you were going for poetic phrasing just now," Kitty retorted, "then you perhaps went too far with it."

"Shut yourself."

"You shut yourself."

"Girls, will you tear my nerves to shreds?" our mother asked. "Your father has only been dead and gone for a month, and you both are already arguing with each other."

"Mary and Kitty both are insensitive to their times of staged arguments," I responded, sarcastic and not sincere. "They do not time them so very well."

"I do not think it wise to consider our arguments as being things that we do for our own amusement," Kitty responded, sullen.

"She meant it as a joke," Mary corrected her. "Why, could you not tell?"

"It's early. My mind is a bit sluggish."

"Your mind is always sluggish."

"And you are ugly."

"Girls, what did I just say?" my mother directed.

Mary and Kitty sat down, ignoring each other.

"Mother, I do not think they shall be forever silenced on this matter," I added, "therefore, we have to entertain the possibility that they will do it again. I can adjust to their bickering, for it would have been something that father was used to."

"Yet, back to my point," our mother snapped. "If Charlotte Collins is to have a child, I suppose that you have a point since you put it like that. However, I still do not know what is more vexing, that you are going to see a friend who has not been especially loyal to you or respectful to our family, or that Jane refuses to go to London now and stay with the Gardiners."

When hearing this news, my head shot towards Jane.

Jane was not going to go to London? Yet, if she remained, then there was no chance of her seeing Mr. Bingley again!

CHAPTER 2

JANE, THE MOVABLE

"*J*ane?" I repeated. "Is this true?"

"Well, yes," Jane whispered, stitching even more at her needlework. "I thought it was best."

"But it is not!" our mother declared passionately. "If there is one time that is best to seek out Mr. Bingley, no time would be better than the present. For if Charlotte is with child, and it turns out that it is a boy, then we shall be homeless if she decides to take over Longbourn. Therefore, our situation is most painful, and the urgency is pressing. You must marry, Jane. And Mr. Bingley shall be the one to save us all."

"But our father has just passed away," Jane retorted. "Is it not indelicate, Mama, for me to be traveling to town so soon after his passing? It would seem like I lack all proper feelings that a daughter is owed to her father, as well as my actions may appear as mercenary."

"If your father were here, then he would agree with me."

"Would he, Mama?" I asked, still sitting in my father's chair. "Would he, truly?"

"I was the one who was married to him for over twenty years."

"No doubt, you are the expert on our father's mind and mood, but Jane has a right to remain at Longbourn."

"And yet, you are not," our mother pointed out. "You are leaving the family behind to see to your friend."

"What Lizzy does is different, due to the purity of intention," Mary supported me, lowering her book. "For Charlotte is in our predicament as well and Mr. Collins was also our kinsman. Therefore, her leaving to go to Hunsford is a proper duty that does not impose itself upon the weight of grieving for our father."

"She is going to save our family," our mother continued, "and Jane, by going to London, you shall do the same. Your father did not breathe his last breath for us to lay down and die along with him. No. He would have desired that we kept on living and maintaining this family."

Suddenly, Jane stood up, dropping her needlework in the process. I went to assist her, but she cleaned it up too swiftly for me to help.

"I beg your pardon," Jane apologized, "you must excuse me."

Jane left the room and went upstairs to her bedroom.

"I have a letter to compose," I said, "therefore, you must excuse me as well."

I went to the door and then had another idea.

"Mama, where is Lydia?"

"Oh, she is with Mrs. Forster, who requested her particular company because she desired her advice on a certain matter."

I turned to Kitty, who looked down at the bonnet that she was making up. She began to sew faster.

"I would recommend, Mama," I requested, "that in the future, when she visits Mrs. Forster, to make certain that Kitty is still with her."

"I think I know how to look after you all, pray. Lydia is fine with Mrs. Forster. You need to learn to trust your sisters. With there being a simple *tête à tête* between two women, what could be dangerous?"

"I cannot speak from your perspective, Mama. For quite frankly, I have seen some *tête à têtes'* end with both women trying each other's patience to such a degree that they secretly wished to proceed to kick and throw each other out of the room. Now, I shall leave before either of you feel that way towards myself."

Turning my heel, I left the room.

As I walked up the steps, my mind quickly rushed over the

events that had occurred in the past few months. Such an eventful life we had led for country folk who lived in a small village. As is the way of the mind, your thoughts scanned the events in a quick succession of a chain of events—events which did not appear to be connected at the time yet were connected all the same.

Five months ago, we had learned the news that Netherfield Park was let. With it being a sizeable and impressive estate, the renter proved to be a man of property. It was Mr. Charles Bingley, a man of great fortune.

He came into Hertfordshire, and *Change* came with him. For he had brought a company with him, consisting of his two older sisters Caroline Bingley and Louisa Hurst. Two gentlemen were in the company as well: Mr. Hurst, who was Louisa's husband, and Mr. Fitzwilliam Darcy of Pemberly, Derbyshire. Mr. Hurst was a man of little consequence to my memories, for he was a man more of fashion than wealth or intellect.

And then there was Mr. Darcy!

Despite his attempts for the reverse, he was the sort of character who had rested in the depths of the mind because one never desired him to. Tall, handsome, striking…and the proudest and most disagreeable man in the whole of my acquaintance! We met the company at an assembly, where he slighted me in the worst conceivable manner. He was Mr. Bingley's bosom friend. And he was my permanent enemy.

As time progressed, Jane and I had two different experiences with both men.

Mr. Bingley, from all appearances, had fallen in love with her.

Mr. Darcy, from all appearances, had fallen into disdain with me.

The contrast of both friends to each of us sisters was like night versus day. Yet as the days rolled on, both emotions became stronger on all accounts. Mr. Bingley's emotions of affection seemed to increase with my sister. And Mr. Darcy's animosity towards me became ever fixed.

The same could be said of Mr. Bingley's sisters. Caroline and Louisa loved Jane and despised me to such a degree that they perhaps wished me to be on the other side of the world.

As Mr. Bingley's attentions toward my sister increased, we were all convinced that a wedding was to approach soon after. This theory was well-fixed upon our minds to such a point, that when Mr. Bingley had held a ball at his estate, Netherfield Park, we secretly regarded it as the beginnings to the sincere discussion of a permanent alliance being formed between them.

It would have been a marriage completely worth the earning!

It would have been the crowning achievement to our mother's ambitions, for her principal aim in life was to get us all married, and the sole chief consolation that often made up for when that didn't happen, was always hearing the news and gossip from other women in the neighborhood.

Mr. Bingley was in love with Jane, I was sure.

At the Netherfield ball that apparent connection was confirmed when he danced with her for three dances. Such a marked attention ought to have spoken for itself!

I recalled it all with perfect clarity, for that ball offered me little to no internal pleasure, for all the dance offered was two dances with my dreaded cousin, Mr. Collins, and was soon followed by a marriage proposal that I had to reject. The second negative aspect was that the one man who I had wished to dance with, Mr. George Wickham, had not attended the ball. And then there was the third element of the ball that also added to my woes—Mr. Darcy himself!

Mr. Darcy, Mr. Darcy, Mr. Darcy!

The man who antagonized me so. It was lamentable already that I had no choice but to despise him forever. From his pride, conceit, that was—I would never deny—shown apparent to me from the very beginning of his rudeness towards myself and others, left me to feel my resentment to his person very keenly.

Yet, this was all augmented by the history that I had learned that Mr. Darcy had with Mr. Wickham. The history between both men was fantastic, tragic, with Mr. Darcy being the villain, and Mr. Wickham being the victim who lost much in life because of Mr. Darcy's pride. How could such a man be worked on?

And then, for Mr. Darcy to accost me at the ball, requesting my hand to dance! This marked attention only enraged me further, and when the dance was done, I left the floor, confused. I was set to despise him when we danced. Yet, when I was done, I did not hate him. To this moment, I could not explain it. It hardly seemed rational, but I daresay that I only temporarily wondered at him. I did not care for him either. Yet I just…did not know what to make of him and his stern scowl by the time that the dance was done.

For that was another contrast to the many differences that Mr. Darcy and Mr. Bingley had with each other—one was simple to understand, while the other was complicated.

Mr. Bingley was simple, and I could withstand that sort of simplicity. For it was easy to make out his character and sketch his personal outline.

After the ball, it was easy to predict that he would soon propose. With complete certainty, we awaited his coming to Longbourn to put his thoughts of matrimony to completion—and that would be a completion that would *never* come to pass.

Rather, the response that we would get instead from Netherfield Park was a miserable letter from Mr. Bingley's sister, Caroline Bingley, stating that the entire Netherfield party had left the estate, gone back to town, and had no intention of returning again.

I didn't believe it. I told Jane that Mr. Bingley would return for her.

I waited. She waited. We all waited. And that day never came. Therefore, I had to confront the fact that I was in error. Mr. Bingley quit Netherfield, and when he did so, he also seemed to quit any thoughts of my sister from his heart. He never came back for her.

Mr. Collins proposed to me the day after the ball, and I rejected him. Turning his attentions from me, in the hardest of swings, he shifted his gaze elsewhere toward my friend, Charlotte Lucas. She accepted him. And just like that, the fate of Longbourn was sealed.

Yet, the woes that this new alliance had set down had been short-lived. For less than a few months into their marriage, Mr. Collins died suddenly of pitiful causes. And his demise fell right upon the heels of when our father had passed away as well.

One tragedy befell the other. And both Longbourn and Hunsford parsonage lost their masters.

Now, here I was, walking upstairs to offer solace to my sister, who, despite her serene countenance, was heartbroken.

It was moments like this where I was content that I had never fallen in love.

When reaching her room, I knocked on her door.

"Is it you, Lizzy?" Jane asked.

"'Tis I."

"Come in."

I opened the door, entered and then shut the door behind me.

"I could tell it was you," Jane said, removing a shawl from her closet. "Your knock has a particular sound to it."

"Well, I shall have to work on that," I smiled gently, sitting down on her bed. "I would lament the idea of anything I do being predictable or too familiar."

She smiled, and then she sat down at the rocking chair that was by the window.

"Jane," I began, "why are you not going to London?"

"I should have thought you would know my motive," she answered, "and concur with it. Lizzy, our father has just left us. It is highly improper and highly indelicate for me to be going to town now."

"If you go to town, then you would be with our aunt and uncle. You would be amongst family, and they could offer you comfort for the loss we have suffered."

"London is associated as the place where people go to seek diversion and pleasures. I would be called out to spoil if I were to go."

"We've been home for weeks since we lost him. And we have spent every day thinking about him and how he has left us in the place where we are. I do not believe that he would have wanted our souls to die along with his. Yet rather, he would want us to keep going, strengthen ourselves, and push onward. Besides, by going to Cheapside, our aunt and uncle would be delightful company. Nothing could be more natural than to visit relatives when you are grieving. Yet, if you think this way, then you must despise me. For I am leaving for Hunsford myself."

"You are leaving because our friend has lost her husband, and she wants you to visit her and help her return home. That is you leaving for a selfless reason. I would be leaving for selfish ones. Besides, I cannot leave our mother now."

"Our mother will be as she is whether you leave, or you stay."

"But Lizzy, do you think that the household will be able to maintain any sort of equilibrium with both of us gone? Our state is fragile, and with our father gone, there is little left to ensure that all will be well if we both were to be gone at the same time."

This was a point which I, in my carelessness, had overlooked.

"Oh," I sighed, "yes, I had not thought of that. Perhaps we can entreat upon our Aunt Phillips to inquire after the household every day, and then for our Uncle Phillips to take on the role of father while we are away. He is a resourceful man and does have some consideration for us. Therefore, perhaps, if we allow him to rise to the occasion, he might be a proper substitute."

"Oh, yes." Jane smiled. "I had not thought of that. Now I feel as if I am the foolish one. Yes, we can entreat him."

"I shall visit him on the morrow. But Jane, let us be candid while also willing to speak plainly. I know why you truly do not wish to go to London."

"I am certain that I do not know what you mean," she responded, standing up and going to the window.

"You know precisely what I refer to," I pressed. "You are afraid of going there, with the express fear of appearing as if you are chasing after Mr. Bingley."

My direct approach disarmed her, and her cheeks developed a rosy hue.

"Let us speak in truths, Jane," I said, "for the hour is growing late."

"When you say the lateness of the hour, do you refer to ourselves, or our father's fate?"

"Both. For I feel a change in me. The loss of our father has taught me to feel how temporary our state is in life, we are not going to live forever. Life, as our father has proven, is short. Perhaps I am done with being indirect, for what good has it done to either of us? As much as I despise the choice that Charlotte made with her alliance, I am not such a blockhead to ignore that she was successful in one way, she showed much affection, and not less, and it caught her a husband. You do not wish to go to London, because, in the eyes of the world, it would look as if you are chasing after Mr. Bingley. And you do not desire to be called out to spoil, exposed to the world for chasing after a man."

"Lizzy, how could I not be afraid of being presented in such an image? If I were to go to London, then I would be exposed, my character would be fixed as that being of a woman who is pursuing a man that does not love her."

"I believe that Mr. Bingley loves you."

"If he loved me...then, Lizzy, he would have returned. And he would have made me an offer. As such, whatever affection he may have possessed for me, it was either of a passing inclination or that he did not truly care for me."

"He did care. It was not disinterested notice that he gave you, but rather, it was true partiality. His reasons for not ever returning to Netherfield Park may always have been, as I had concluded before, under the influence of his sisters and the proud Mr. Darcy. After all, *they* had no particular regard for our family."

"Lizzy, you know that I believe that Caroline is incapable of any ill treatment towards me. She was right to write to me, warning me of Mr. Bingley's lack of consideration for me truly."

"And I believe that her words were that of a scheming cow."

"Lizzy!"

"Forgive me, but I must speak plain again. If she is your true friend, then why has she not written? Why has she not responded to any of your last letters?"

"I cannot give you an answer."

"Because there is none. While I do not deny that Mr. Bingley ought to be his own master, sometimes, we humans are easily influenced by stronger wills around us, and Mr. Bingley does rely on Mr. Darcy's advice. And Mr. Darcy, who is of the taciturn and bitter disposition, where he was willing to rob Mr. Wickham of his inheritance, is capable of turning the reputation of innocent people into disfavor. We aren't rich. We aren't a family that moves in the same circles as the ton. We are lowly in Mr. Darcy's eyes, and Mr. Bingley, while he ought to be guided by himself, is perhaps guided by his stubborn friend. Mr. Darcy is immovable. And Mr. Bingley is always on the move. But, if you were to go to London, then there is the possibility that you may see him, while not under Mr. Darcy's stern gaze. You could meet Mr. Bingley on your own terms. I understand the desire to not pursue a man who has not pursued you. Yet I think that you may do your soul good by attempting it."

"How can I find goodness in it? I do not wish to be disagreeable, for you are speaking from such a great intellect, but I must ask."

"Jane, are you happy, sitting here and not doing anything to change your life?"

"My family is all that I need. I have you, therefore, I am content."

"But you are not. You are in pain. The loss of Mr. Bingley has altered your happiness. And the reason that it has is because you are in love with him."

"Lizzy," Jane sighed, "do not judge my harsh speech, for I know that it shall come from the heart of a woman who is emotionally distraught. I am foolish for loving a man when it is never proper to like a man unless he finds you agreeable already. And I am forced to be here, having no idea what to do. For any action of any kind, would be an error."

"And to not act would be worse. I believe…that your heart will never fully rest until you have decided to do something about it. By going to London and visiting the Bingley townhouse, you will have done something while still being innocent of your actions. But if you do nothing and you give up, then you will always spend the rest of your life wondering what could have been if you decided to act. Which is worse to you, risking the world making fun of you or never taking that chance and possibly going to see him?"

I offered her this dilemma. And if I knew my sister, then there was only one answer she would give.

"It would be wrong of me to leave when our father has recently been gone."

"I miss him. I miss him always. But as I said, we can miss him and still live our lives. He raised us to be able to continue on, and we shall."

Jane looked forward and took my hand.

"Lizzy, thank you for convincing me," she said. "I will go to London."

I laughed.

"All may fall apart," she said and laughed nervously.

"That is what love is."

"Oh." She wrapped her arms around me, and we embraced.

Then it was time to leave her be, so I left her room, giving her time to reflect on her own musings and romantic dreams.

Walking down the steps, I went to the sitting room and spoke to my mother.

"She will go to London," I assured her. "You have something to hope for. Unless it all will come to nothing, of course."

Without waiting for her reply, I went to the hall and prepared myself for my daily walk.

"Of course, it can all come to something," our mother called. "Remember that man who once wrote Jane those pretty verses? If a man can write poetry about you, then another man can easily fall in love with you. Mark my words now, we are saved. We are saved!"

Suddenly Kitty raced into the hall.

"Lizzy, are you walking to Meryton?" Kitty asked.

"Aye."

"I wish to visit our Aunt Phillips. Can you wait for me to join you?"

"Be quick."

"Yes."

Yet, like a moth to a flame, my mind was driven back into the comforts of the past—for memories, like the taunting ghosts of shadows' past, have the ever-powerful ability to rise up in our minds and fill our present thought.

Indeed!

How much of our present days were spent by living in the past! And, when thinking from that mindset, from the perspective of someone who was always turning around and looking to their history rather than turning forward and facing what lies ahead, it makes one ponder the query: are any of us ever fully living?

Suddenly, this revelation seized my faculties. The emotion, the sensation, was so very overwhelming that it sparked my instincts. A fire was lit from within me as I raced down the stairs, went to my father's study again, and I laid down on the floor. With my arms stretched out, I looked up at the ceiling.

"Father," I whispered aloud, "wherever you are, can you see me? Can you see us from the lofty height that you are perched on? Or from the rocks beneath that you lay under? Wherever you go, no matter the height, I pray you may hear me. I shall love you forever, and I miss you terribly. Yet, onward I will go. I will not use your memory as a weight to hold me down. Yet rather, on the wings of your soul, I shall rise up. Never shall I let this sadness oppress my will. I will keep going. I shall keep my best at maintaining this family. And for your soul, I shall make certain that we keep Longbourn. This we owe you."

When done offering my message to the soul that had left Longbourn and gone into the afterlife, I rose up and left the room, joined Kitty, and we began to walk to Meryton.

As we walked, we reached a hill that was near my home, and another memory had seized me. It was a strange thing to recollect. When the Netherfield party had quitted the estate and fled to town, the last face that I had seen was not Mr. Bingley or his sisters. Rather, it had belonged to Mr. Darcy.

On the day of their departure, I had been walking in the garden of our estate at Longbourn. As I had been walking, I felt the presence of someone else nearby. When I turned, I saw Mr. Darcy a distance away, sitting atop his horse and looking down on our home.

At first, I looked away. I wished to defy him to the best of my ability. Yet, his gaze drew my curiosity. Turning back, I looked at him once more, and he was still there, looking at our grounds from his lofty position, as well as staring at me. Still on his horse, he did not move one muscle. Both he and I continued to stare at each other, one refusing to tear the gaze from the other. We were challenging each other, and I was more than happy to oblige with that challenge.

I knew his scheme. For if he looked on me with disdain often, then naturally, he was coming to find fault with the smallness of our estate compared to how his might look. He came to ridicule, to belittle our fortunes. His pride showed in his eyes as he continued to look at me.

Showing that I would not let him unnerve me, I continued to pick flowers to place in our home. Yet the hateful man would not move at all for a time. It really made me despise him so.

What could he be about in this scheme of his? He was leaving, and Mr. Bingley was going to be leaving with him. And the Bingley sisters despised us well enough already. Therefore, why could he not triumph over us at a distance and be satisfied?

No! He had to see his sordid work. He had to relish in it. Oh, hateful man!

Eventually, I went to one of the backdoors to our home and took one last glance at him before I entered. I stared defiantly at him. Yet, this did not deter his stern and quizzical brow. He returned my glare with one of his own, and this would perhaps be as it always would be with us.

Yet, I would learn that this would be something I would never have to worry over again. For the Netherfield party had quit the estate, and it was now fixed that they would remain in London for the entire winter.

"So," Kitty announced, which dug right through my thoughts and musings, "Lizzy, I must ask you something."

"What do you wish to know?"

"Mrs. Forster is dining with Lydia now, but she did not invite me. Is it not fair, do you think? For I am two years older than Lydia, and...do I make myself disagreeable? I thought I was just as good-humored as Lydia, but I feel as if I am often fading into obscurity. I just...it is not fair."

I smiled.

"I am sorry for you," I allowed.

"You are?"

"Yes. For you are at that stage in life where you have no choice but to wonder what everyone is thinking of you. Do you ever find yourself attempting to base your character around what you assume is what everyone prefers your character to be?"

"Yes!" Kitty responded, a little loudly, but she quieted down afterwards. I did not censure her outburst, because no one was around us, and I saw that her response came from a proper place of satisfaction of being able to voice what she was truly feeling. "Yes, I do. I desire to please, but for some reason or other, I do not know where I stand with anyone."

"I once heard someone say something that I do believe I am beginning to learn myself. For it is the lesson that can occur when one has reached four and twenty. They said that when you are in your teenage years, during the trying time, you are always worried about what people are thinking of you, so you change your disposition every half an hour to accommodate their maxims. Then when you reach the middle of your twenties, at my age, you cease to care what others are saying about you. Yet, when you reach your fifties, you have the grandest epiphany, you realize that no one was looking at you to begin with."

"That is unpleasant," Kitty whined, "because that would imply we had to reach old age before we have any peace of mind. I do not want to wait. I desire peace right now. And we never fully obtain it."

"I do not think absolute peace is something that can ever be obtained. If it were so, then our father would still be alive."

Kitty gave me a look.

"I am sorry for what you are going through, Lizzy."

"You are going through it as well."

"Well yes..." she hesitated, and then she continued, "and well...no." This surprised me, and I looked at her sharply. The change of my countenance alarmed her, I could see, and she immediately tried to remedy this by softening the truth. "What I mean is, I do miss him. I loved our father...yet I am not certain that he loved me."

"Oh," I allowed, "Kitty, that manner of thought is not fully sound. Our father did care for you."

"He only looked to me to find fault, and you know it. Therefore, how was I to bestow affection for someone who never showed it much for me? I sound evil, I know. Mind you, I did love him, and I miss his being in his study. Yet I cannot miss anything else—or is my speech confusing?"

"I understand your meaning. Our father did care. He simply had a sardonic sort of humor, and that was his way of showing affection for us. That was his manner of showing that he cared."

"You understood him more than I did."

"I had the pleasure of being born with the same comprehension of mindset. You are like Mother, so you draw closer to her. It is natural. Also, our father had one thing not on his side."

"And what is that?"

"The more I look back on his behavior, I believe he was a man who believed that he had all the time in the world. While our mother often spoke of the unpredictable but inevitable hour of his demise, I do not believe he considered it. Or rather, his mind rejected the notion of it. That is only natural, for none of us view ourselves as mortal, despite all the evidence that we are such."

"That is true. I feel as if I will live forever."

"And I wish that we could. Perhaps, so did he. Therefore, he did not comprehend that time was not always his greatest ally, supposing he had more of it and not less of it. I think he thought he had more time to show his love for you, for all of us, before he left. But time cut him shorter than he assumed it would, and he died before he could administer his true affection for us all. Thus, I believe, you are another one of the regrets he passed away with having."

"Are you saying that because you know for certain? Or because you wish to spare my feelings?"

"I did not ask him when he left us behind, so what can I say that can ever be certain?"

"True. Thank you for saying it nevertheless."

We walked to Meryton, and Kitty spoke to a few of the officers as we progressed to Aunt Phillip's home.

CHAPTER 3

HEARTS DIVIDED

*I*n the heart of Canter's Abbey, an estate where one of the wealthiest families in Britain lived, there was a large party occurring on the grounds and in other parts of the home. The house belonged to the Grangers, who resided in Cranford just near the village of Wiltshire. Being the large estate that was attached to the quaint village, it was the estate that offered distinction among the county and helped solidify Cranford's identity, keeping it from being a place of little consequence.

Sir Aleck Granger was the head of the estate, having inherited a luxurious house, four miles, including farmland for a large set of tenants, as well as twelve thousand pounds a year. Sir Aleck was a mixture of aristocratic sophistication and jovial manners that belonged to provincial people. He was wealthy... so he knew precisely what he could get away with when lacking the refinement of the ton, because between his rank, wealth, family's name and annual Bonfire Night celebrations, he could get away with what he wished. Also, the fact that he was a single man of large fortune, only at the age of thirty, and had an overall pleasing appearance added to his manifold attractions, added to his charms. He was a man who was not terribly handsome, but still pleasing to look at, and therefore, his looks rested between the two extremes of extremely handsome and average.

However, men such as him held much power and influence

amongst the ton, and when he called for his annual Bonfire Night, Mr. Fitzwilliam Darcy of Pemberly was one of the many who responded.

And this was the situation that Mr. Charles Bingley found himself in, as he stood alone in the privacy of the library at the estate. Being bosom friends with the legendary Mr. Darcy of Pemberly had many more benefits to it than drawbacks. When long ago, Mr. Darcy and Mr. Bingley found themselves tossed into each other's company, and even more, discovering that they genuinely liked each other, each had much to gain from the camaraderie. Mr. Darcy gained a friend who was loyal, accepting of his often taciturn or sardonic disposition, and Mr. Bingley innocently gained a friend who was one of the most respected men in Britain. Often, Bingley found himself welcomed in circles that would be a benefit to his prosperity. And his sisters, Miss Caroline Bingley and Mrs. Hurst, also enjoyed the fruits of the connection.

It was this same connection that allowed the entire Bingley family to be permitted to join Mr. Darcy at Canter's Abbey, where they would be Sir Aleck's special guests, and they would be able to enjoy the festivities that were on the estate.

Outside, over two hundred guests had come, from both occupants from the neighboring gentry estates, some less illustrious persons who lived in Cranford, and some others of the ton who always especially traveled to Wiltshire to enjoy the night.

Each year, Sir Aleck would invite many of the best families in London, allowing over thirty of them to stay in his home, and the others would remain at the inns in Cranford.

This sort of arrangement always suited the Cranford villagers because it was this annual party that would lead to much business coming to the Cranford shops, and they would get the chance to meet new people.

Sir Aleck, who was the county's magistrate, was a benevolent neighbor who did not find it below himself to get to know the lowliest residents. Therefore, whenever he held the Bonfire Night festivities, everyone knew that London's least snobby aristocratic members were going to come among them for at least a week's time and enjoy the quaintness of the country. Sometimes, some of the wealthier families were so social they would remain in Cranford for two weeks or three, and the inns, taverns, dressmakers and craftsmen delighted in the flattery that it did the place.

These pleasures were not one-sided, for the London ton would go into Wiltshire knowing that they were regarded as exotic and therefore fervently worshiped by the lower classes that made up the villagers. As such, rather than turning their noses up at the Cranford villagers, the ton found that they had more to gain by moving amongst them. The passionate admiration that the country folk had for them was able to swell their vanity, appeal to their pride, and renew the certainty of their superiority over a large portion of England. After all, amongst themselves, they could be cold or superficial to each other, always feeling as if they were competing. Yet, when among those who were lesser, they were like stars to be wondered at and had no reason to feel resentment towards them.

Thus, Mr. Darcy felt this was the perfect diversion for the state in which Mr. Bingley found himself. For, ever since they had left Hertfordshire, Mr. Darcy had hoped the distance would diminish Mr. Bingley's feelings for Jane Bennet and his original designs toward her.

At first, Mr. Darcy's proscription for Mr. Bingley's predicament was to deliver him back to the London aristocracy, where many other women were better suited for a man like his friend. This was the same idea that Bingley's sisters had as well. Unfortunately, the reverse had occurred. Every woman introduced to Mr. Bingley did not reach his heart. In faith, she did not even reach his thoughts! This strong preference towards Miss Jane Bennet alarmed Mr. Darcy, who did want to see his friend happy.

Time past, and soon the calendar fell on November, and Mr. Darcy realized that his old acquaintance, Sir Aleck Granger, was once more hosting his annual Bonfire Night celebration.

This was the perfect arrangement!

Canter's Abbey, Sir Aleck and the holiday always brought out the best of everyone who went there. The women of the ton, who had often been confined to the restricted manners of the aristocracy, now would loosen themselves and become artless. Artlessness was precisely what Mr. Bingley needed. Women, who did not walk around with any particular designs, were ideal for both of them. And because of such, this rendered the women more attractive. There was even one time where Mr. Darcy fancied himself in love there once when he had come a few years ago.

Mr. Bingley and his sisters, always unable to resist such a glorious opportunity to socialize and enjoy themselves, agreed. Mr. Darcy requested that Sir Aleck extend the invitation to include his friends, Sir Aleck was amenable to the idea, and therefore, they had come into Wiltshire, where they were met by Sir Aleck with an open nature and a congenial air.

Mr. Darcy was at his best—well, as good as his nature could be when he was not at Pemberly.

And Mr. Bingley was overjoyed at first.

The Bonfire celebration was delightful. A huge tent had been set up along the grounds, huge bonfires were lit, and magnificent fireworks were released, standing out against the night sky. All were once more filled with spirits, celebrating the anniversary of the Gunpowder Plot when Guy Fawkes and others failed to blow up King James I and Parliament, and Fawkes was found hiding gunpowder in the basement.

The night had been delightful, until one Lord and Lady Chatterley had shown up late to the festivities. When they arrived, Lady Chatterley removed her warm shawl, and it was revealed that she had sprinkled her muslin gown with drops of water and perfume. As such, it clung to her person which proved scandalous to some of the guests.

This was enough to unnerve Mr. Darcy, alarm his sensibilities and drive him to distraction. He could not believe she would be so indelicate as to commit such behavior in so public a display.

It was in this moment that he saw Mr. Bingley retreat inside the estate, and he did not blame him. Retreating inside as well, Mr. Darcy followed his friend and soon came upon him in the library looking out over the grounds, watching the celebration from within.

"Darcy?" Mr. Bingley replied, seeing his friend enter from over his shoulder. "Do not worry. I am quite well."

"I know you are."

"I just needed a moment away from the enthusiastic crowd."

"I never knew you to be one who enjoys time away from gaiety. However, given the circumstances, I can understand why you sought refuge. I, too, am enraged over that public display of vulgarity."

"Oh, you are referring to Lady Chatterley's arriving with her gown sprinkled in water?"

"Of course. Mark my words, Bingley, I never encountered such impropriety on my previous visits to Canter's Abbey."

"That is not what disturbed me," Mr. Bingley replied. "You know that such actions as that do not alarm me. Besides, this is Bonfire Night. We are celebrating the unsuccessful attempts of Guy Fawkes's plot to blow up King and Parliament. More scandalous things have happened in history than a woman coming to a celebration with water sprinkled on her gown."

"The gown is muslin, and it clings to her person now."

"She is wearing undergarments. I shall survive it all, I daresay. On closer reflection, such behavior does put all manners of behavior into a sharper perspective, does it not? Among the ton, we have a woman who sprinkled her gown to have it cling to her person, and now we are celebrating the day when a man failed at blowing up King James I. It puts lesser offensive actions under a less fine harshness of view. It makes one realize that sometimes we are too severe on each other."

The two of them were friends for so long they learned to read between the lines of the words sometimes spoken between them. Judging from his friend's philosophical speech and his morose demeanor, Darcy knew his friend was alluding to something else.

"When you speak of such," Darcy observed, "I presume you refer to a different subject entirely."

"Perhaps I do."

"Charles, are you thinking of Miss Jane Bennet now?"

"Yes, I am. Yes, I do still."

Darcy closed his eyes for a second. It was a bitter thing, although he knew that this conversation was only a matter of time in coming.

"I shall drive you mad," Bingley continued. "I know that I shall. Yet please, let me speak."

"I do not attempt to silence you."

"I thank you for your counsel, and I believe you to be correct, Jane did not care for me. She found my company pleasing and perhaps no more than that. But that revelation does not, nor ever, successfully diminish the feelings on my side. I think... Darcy, I think that I was truly in love with her. And I still am, perhaps. I thought coming here would prove to be a most excellent diversion, and it would take my mind away. Diversions have helped me recover from heartaches in the past, but this is different. Each time that I speak to a woman, I think of Jane. I see her with my waking eyes. She is always there. And the foolish behavior of her mother and some of her younger sisters... is it truly any more vulgar than what a member of our circle has done in arriving at Bonfire Night with her dress sprinkled with water?"

"You compare both events in an attempt to justify having Mrs. Bennet as a mother-in-law?"

"Mrs. Bennet did not ever try and blow up Parliament and James I by storing gunpowder in the basement either."

"No, she did not. Although between the total want of propriety on her part, her younger daughters, and even on occasion, her husband, their behavior would blow up your family's good name on every opportunity that was given. I will always advise you against it, for you shall diminish and lose all that your father strove for you to gain."

"But does it always follow that a woman or man should be punished because of the family they were born into?"

"You very well are aware that was not my primary concern. It was not, nor ever, their lack in refined manners the chief criticism I lay at Miss Jane Bennet's figurative door. It is her lack of partiality to you which I feel I have seen. If I knew she was fully in love with you, then perhaps I might have hesitated to advise you to quit Netherfield and abandon her as a prospect. But your sisters and I all saw the same scene, you loved her, that was certain and true. She, on the other hand, received your attentions with the compliment of being flattered. She enjoyed your pleasing attentions, but she never displayed any peculiar regard for you. When in love, we humans seek out one another. We feel a strong desire to be beside them always, to the point where, despite our initial education, we impose ourselves on the public and display our feelings, unguarded."

"Women are trained not to display their feelings."

"I've seen women and men in love, and when it is a true love, they forget that rule easily. Miss Jane Bennet always remembered that rule. If she always had such presence of mind and control of temper, then she has the benefits of keeping her mind but never losing her heart. Love...love leads to one losing their heart, despite the outcome."

"You've never mentioned it so eloquently before."

"Eloquence was not taught at Cambridge."

Bingley chuckled.

"So, what do I do with these feelings?" Bingley asked, innocently. "These painful feelings? I wish I could forget her."

"Do not even attempt to," Darcy offered. This advice surprised Bingley, for he expected his friend to say something more... standard and logical.

"Do not?"

"No. Because the more you attempt not to care for her, the more you shall. Time has taught me that sad truth. Accept that you love her, but that you shall enjoy your life anyway. And you shall. Then you will be able to be as you once were, moving among ladies of our acquaintance... and rather than seeing the woman that they *are not*, you shall see the women that they *are*. Time is your ally. Respect her for it."

"Thank you," Bingley smiled, "that may be the best advice that you have ever given me."

"I have my moments."

Both friends were suddenly interrupted when Sir Aleck entered with his jovial nature, immediately bringing a lightness to the room. That there were few men whom Mr. Darcy knew for which he could tolerate with equanimity was a well-known fact, but fortunately Sir Aleck was one of those men. He did not possess an intimate relationship with Darcy, but they had an easy acquaintance where neither asked much of the other. And that was all that Mr. Darcy was happy to oblige.

"There you both are!" Sir Aleck boomed—yet his bold declarations were always of the sort that contained much grace within them. There was something about his air and manner which left very little to reprove, even if his behavior ever bordered along the lines of needing reproving. "Hiding from the festivities, I see? Or am I wrong, and it is from scandal?"

"I hope that you sent Mrs. Chatterley back to the inn that her husband allowed her to escape from," Mr. Darcy responded.

"Of course, I did no such thing," Sir Aleck responded. "Forgive my gentleness of temper at this time, but it did not border along the lines of implacable resentment. Nay, I merely had my sister gently accost her, laugh mockingly, and then pull her along to a guestroom where she would offer her a different gown to put on. I firmly believed that if we made light of the affair, then Mrs. Chatterley's reputation would not be razed when she returned to town."

"You were too soft," Mr. Darcy advised.

"Was I? And I take it that you are about to prescribe the Darcy remedy?"

"And that remedy might very well be sending the lady away and exposing her to the center of perpetual gossip?" Mr. Bingley smiled at his taciturn friend.

"A woman who shows up at Bonfire Night, or any night for that matter," Mr. Darcy continued, "with her muslin gown sprinkled with water, is asking to be met with the cold glares of the ton."

"Yes, she ought to be condemned forever," Sir Aleck responded, "there is no room for foolishness or a want of propriety. Well, Darcy, I have the benefit of this being my home and allowing myself to be a little more lenient on the follies of others, as long as those follies do not lead to the world coming undone. Now, you make me forget my purpose in coming. Mr. Bingley, man, your sisters are looking for you."

Mr. Bingley sighed.

"Why? They see me every day."

"They wish to have you meet an acquaintance of theirs."

"And by theirs, they mean another woman who I have no desire to meet."

With his energy deflating slightly, Bingley left the room.

———

Watching Mr. Bingley's retreating form, Sir Aleck quickly began to make deductions. Once he and Mr. Darcy were fully alone, Sir Aleck turned to Darcy, his eyes keen and his expression prepared to begin to disassemble a situation that he knew little about.

"I have never seen Bingley look that undesirous to meet a woman," Sir Aleck responded. "I have always seen him keen to be tossed into love."

"The practice of being tossed into love has soured on him, I am glad to admit."

"Darcy, not all of us are afraid of getting our hearts broken sometimes. For some of us, it is how evidence bestows itself and gives proof that our hearts are still working."

"You know that I do not bow down to such a practice and make way for it."

"No, but others do, and not everyone is you. And what better, not everyone ought to be anyone else but themselves."

Mr. Darcy arched his eyebrow.

"What are you saying, Aleck?"

"That I believe you have a strong hold over him. I know how strongly he depends on your advice."

"Is there ill in that?"

"You are not frightened by the concept that Bingley's happiness and judgment depend solely on your powers of discernment? I would be very afraid if I were you. Too much power, in that sense, can have dangerous repercussions."

"Such as?"

"It can fold over on itself and find its way back to you. Usually, when a man like Bingley behaves in such a manner, I find that it is often because he either no longer likes the idea of falling in and out of love, or because he is heartbroken. Which is it?"

Darcy half-smiled.

"Aleck, you know very well I shall never break his confidence."

"Too right, too right. Friends must never break confidence with each other, but they should only break bread with each other."

"You're speaking in tongues, Aleck. What game are you about to play?"

"Nothing at all. You know very well that when I play, I often play on words and no more than that. Now, while we really ought to make a truce on you accepting that sometimes my guests aren't perfect, they ought to be forgiven for their occasional folly, and I accept the influence you have over your friend, let us speak more to the point and purpose."

Sir Aleck produced a letter.

"For your eyes only…and for your ever-ongoing luck in finding events that allow you time for quiet contemplation where you can be alone."

"A letter?"

"Yes. Apparently, it should have arrived earlier this week, but the postal service misplaced it. Yet, in their desire to remain upon good standing here at Canter's Abbey, one of the workers was studious enough to bring it here, interrupting his holiday. Good man, that!"

"What?" Darcy responded, taking the letter. "He was perhaps the one who made the mistake to begin with."

"You really must make allowances for people who rectify their mistakes, wholly and completely, once they notice the mistake has been made."

"I will weigh the scales of his rectifying his actions when I analyze this letter. If it was an urgent message, where the news was desperate, then his atonement means little to me."

Darcy looked at the letter and saw it was from Rosings Park, and the writing on the front was in his aunt's own hand.

"Who is it from?" Sir Aleck asked.

"My aunt, Lady Catherine."

"Oh, then it all now becomes quite clear."

Both men looked at each other.

"The letter is full of nonsense," they spoke in unison.

Accepting the large possibility that his aunt's discourse would bear little to no alarm on any subject matter, Mr. Darcy sat down and began to read the letter.

"Shall I leave you to it?" Sir Aleck asked.

"Yes, thank you, Aleck."

Sir Aleck left the room.

Opening the letter, Darcy began to read his aunt's correspondence.

Dearest Fitzwilliam,

You are too much away for very long, and therefore, your presence is required at Rosings Park. My desire for your coming is a natural one, full of disinterestedness on my part, but out of pure concern for your welfare. When you are too long away from the serenity and superior airs of Rosings, I worry for your health and state of mind. Returning here shall give you all the time in the world to recover from the melancholic musings that naturally occur from moving about society and disallowing yourself to have access to the best situation that is Kent.

I know that it shall always be business and the obligations of running an estate that shall be the necessary evils that keep you away. But as your late mother and father knew, your spirits were always deeply affected by the shades of Rosings upon your cheek. For here, you have family that loves you tenderly, and Anne is always inquiring of when you shall return. For only this morning, I declared to her, "you miss your cousin, Anne, do you not?" Her reply was the perfect sort of reaction of sophistication, demureness and composure of countenance. She said nothing at all, and that was as it should be. For all know, when a woman speaks so publicly of her affection, it often means she is professing something that she does not feel. But rather, if she does not speak, she lets the silence speak for itself and confirm that she says yes.

Darcy lowered the letter and rolled his eyes. His aunt's logic was, and always would be, of many confident remarks that were influenced by the power of her own will; she believed something, and therefore, naturally, the rest of the world must believe as she did. For those were the people who shaped the very world that all

moved around in! She was the creature all must orbit. But truly…
Anne felt nothing for him, and he felt nothing for her. Yet, with his
Aunt Catherine, her determination would always see her through,
and Darcy knew his aunt would never believe that the future would
play out any other way than how she designed it to. It hurt him,
inwardly, that he knew, one day, he would have to break her heart.

Returning to the letter, he leaned over and continued to peruse
its contents.

Nevertheless, my desire for your visit is for another motive than
the one that is for your welfare. I inform you now, my parson,
Mr. Collins, has recently died—the stupidity of the man! He had
not been reverend at Hunsford but half a year before he goes up
and dies upon me. I find his predicament hard to forgive when I
recall all the other options which I had in choosing a reverend.
Now, I must do the situation all over again of occupying a
replacement for him. This time, I shall do the task more
thoroughly, and choose one who does not possess the vacancy of
mind to die in so frivolous a manner. Indeed, I am quite put out!
Yet still, the poor man, the poor and late Mr. Collins.

Yet, there is the other situation of his widow, Mrs. Collins,
now having to depart from Hunsford when the time arrives. At
present, she is not in any danger of moving, and I would never
commit to such a removal hastily—no, indeed, that would lack all
propriety, and let it not be said that there is no civility at Rosings
Park. I have not secured the post for reverend as of yet and am
content with the honorable Mr. Ashby to do the services as a
substitute until I am able to choose wisely.

At my humble request, I desire that you come to Rosings at
this time. First, I would like you to be in attendance for when I
interview candidates for the position. After all, it will give you
proper practice to see how to choose a clergyman with care for
Rosings—since this estate is something that will be placed in your
hands one day.

Your dear cousin, the Colonel, shall also be coming at this
time, and you know how much I do so enjoy your company
whenever you both attend at once. Your liveliness when in each

other's company offers a wonderful diversion, and it shall do for Mrs. Collins to have some fine gentlemen in her company. It shall help her spirits recover. It also shall add to my own accomplishments, for in her time of mourning, her father and sister are coming to Hunsford to offer her company at this difficult time. Among the visiting company is a friend of hers that Mrs. Collins had informed me was an acquaintance of yours, Miss Elizabeth Bennet.

Though, by her description, I am certain that you perhaps never had an extensive acquaintance with her, for she seems to be a woman of little importance from a family of even lesser significance in society…

Mr. Darcy put down the letter, unable to attend to anything else. Elizabeth Bennet was coming to Rosings Park!

When seeing Elizabeth's name amongst those listed to go to his aunt's estate to console her friend, Mr. Darcy felt all the perversity of feelings that one experiences when confronted with an emotional attachment to a woman that one does not desire to have romantic designs on.

When Bingley had quitted Netherfield Park, Darcy's departure from it was manifold and plural. Bingley was not the only one in danger, so was Darcy. Both men had secretly found themselves enchanted by the two sisters. Although, those sisters belonged to one of the most unappealing families in Britain. Bingley's heart had chosen Jane Bennet. Darcy's had chosen Elizabeth. Bingley's mind was open to this new attraction, but for Darcy, this could not have been a worse situation for which to find himself.

And time was meant to be Darcy's friend!

As well as space.

Space away from Elizabeth Bennet's fine eyes.

Time away from her charming wit.

But all of time and space was not suitable to allow disinterestedness to grow in the place of his desires.

As he lowered the letter, his mind wandered over to the last time he had seen Elizabeth. It was the day of their departure from Netherfield. Bingley had left the day before, while he, Mr. Hurst,

Mrs. Hurst and Caroline Bingley had left the next day. Knowing that they would depart at the appointed hour, Darcy rode his stallion furtively to the edges of Longbourn, waiting for any sign of Elizabeth Bennet walking about the village, as was her usual want to do.

He had not been long disappointed. In the matter of a quarter of an hour, he spied her light countenance, her beautiful figure and her charming face as she walked along. Then their eyes met—she stared at him.

She had stared at him!

Those eyes of hers arrested him, and he could only look at her and admire her boldness. In that moment, it felt as if their souls had touched. Darcy felt it. Therefore, naturally, Elizabeth must have felt it as well. Darcy was sure of it. He could ride up to her and take her heart if he desired to act on his feelings. Darcy retained his composure, and he forced himself to be released from the spell that she held over him.

He hated himself for ever coming. By doing so, he was tormenting himself. Now he did not desire to leave but rather to ride up to Elizabeth, place her upon his horse, and ride away with her. With the strength of his emotions and station in life, he could return with her to Netherfield and steal happiness with her in his bedroom, and her father would have no choice but to accept Darcy as his new son-in-law. Such beauty would be his wife! And she would be all his, without belonging to any other man. Her eyes would sparkle for him alone.

Darcy had managed to pull himself out from under the spell that Elizabeth's presence had placed on him. Taking one last look at her, he turned his horse around and drove off, over the fields and offering himself as much separation from her as he could.

With the distance he placed between her life and his, he was certain that any connection that was between them would break, along with the power she had over him.

On returning to Netherfield, he expected to feel secure in this.

He did not.

Then he realized that all would be well when they arrived in London.

It was not.

Lastly, he knew that his soul and mind would be fully restored, and his heart would achieve ultimate indifference once he returned to society and eventually Pemberly.

It did not.

Through it all, his mind would still wonder towards her and wonder what she was doing, who she was smiling at, and who would be the source that would offer illumination to her cheeks and sparkle to her dark eyes. In the quiet of his heart, there was no peace, for there was ever a tremor that arose when he considered all this.

But now! With this letter, that tremor was now the earth splitting up underneath him.

Restless, he stood up and began to pace around the room.

He could not go to Rosings Park. It would be utterly preposterous and harmful to his resolve, even though his heart yearned for the opposite. However, his aunt requested it. It would be most uncongenial for him to reject her offer when he was not occupied with any conflict and therefore had no obligations that would remove his ability to oblige her.

Also, was he that weak that he could not withstand Elizabeth's society without tripping over his own resolve to not offer her any sort of courtship? Darcy wanted to believe that his resolve was made of stronger stuff than that!

Besides, in the deepest of his desires, he did want to go. He did wish to see her again, and perhaps this was not such a terrible thing. Why not see her again! Perhaps when they met, something would occur that lessened her image in his eyes. Perhaps he would see that the creature he secretly doted on was no more of an angelic presence than any other mortal woman. Perhaps by seeing her at Rosings, he would see how she was, perhaps overwhelmed by all the grandeur, and was not equal to the society of Kent.

In vain, he hoped for anything. For when in love with someone that one does not desire to be in love with, Darcy did what all of us do: wish that the image of those we love is tarnished by an ugly aspect of their nature we had previously overlooked. No matter how harsh that mindset truly is!

"You are a hypocrite, Darcy!" Darcy said to his own reflection, which he happened to glimpse in a mirror along the wall. Walking up to the mirror, Darcy spoke to himself, "You advised Bingley to relinquish his attentions to one sister, and now here you are, desiring to see the other. Towards him you have been kinder than toward yourself."

Pocketing the letter, he left the room and went out to the festivities.

Moving along the crowd of people, Darcy's eyes fell on every young lady he passed by. Every gentlewoman he saw who possessed any ounce of beauty was duly scrutinized. Darcy wanted to feel a quick emotional attachment to any of them, but it was in vain.

At last, he returned to Bingley's side, where his sisters were nearby, and Caroline was eager to see him.

"Mr. Darcy, you idle fellow," Caroline chided, "for you were within when there were such friends to not abandon when the ceremony is about to reach its highest point."

"I am returned at the right time, I presume?" he asked.

"You always return at the right time. How do you manage it?"

"I move by my own clock and no one else's."

"That is another of your uncommon talents. You have so many talents, I shall never be able to list them all."

"But it is still an eager bit of employment to try one's hand at," Mrs. Hurst said, encouraging her sister's attempts at flirtation.

Mr. Darcy turned to Mr. Bingley, and they both gave each other a *look*. Darcy knew what Caroline was doing. Bingley also knew. Therefore, both men were left as kindred spirits, attached by their knowledge of Caroline's schemes.

Darcy drew close to Bingley and whispered in his ear.

"Soon, I shall have to part ways with you."

"You cannot stand my sister's attentions that much?" Bingley retorted.

"I am large enough to survive her flattery. It is my aunt. She has called on me to come to her estate. I will come and visit you all again in two months' time."

"Nothing is wrong, is it?"

"This is Bonfire Night, Charles, nothing is ever wrong on Bonfire Night."

"Stand alert," Mrs. Hurst laughed, "here comes Guy Fawkes. Mr. Hurst, what do you think of it?"

"What?" Mr. Hurst asked, not listening. His wife rolled her eyes and looked away from him. Always content with his wife forgetting his existence, Mr. Hurst returned to seizing a cup of hard cider from a servant who was passing by with mugs of the drink on his tray.

Mr. Darcy had no external reaction, but his mind was falling back on what it always determined when he glimpsed Mr. and Mrs. Hurst. As a match, they were complete with both being equally dissatisfied with each other, each indifferent to the other's happiness and perhaps forever spending their marriage sleeping in different bedrooms. And perhaps they would only become one when having an heir was a necessary thing to make—then again, was it necessary?

It was alliances such as these that made Darcy's concept of marriage a motionless consideration. He thought of having a wife, but never desired it in the end. Since, due to the stress of marriage in life, he had seen more unhappy marriages than happy ones, and he was afraid that, in his desire for the former, he would receive the latter. Therefore, moving slowly was always ideal.

They were all distracted as some of the servants came forward with an effigy, a scarecrow of Guy Fawkes, and they carried it through the crowd.

In the center of the festival, Sir Aleck Granger stood. The servants handed the effigy to their master, and Sir Aleck took it with much applause.

"Guy Fawkes!" Sir Aleck called. "One of a group who tried to blow up Parliament."

The crowd jeered.

"The fool," Sir Aleck grinned, "you can't blow up a King, because there is always a third cousin of his, twice removed, who is dying to take his place and do all the things the first king was planning on doing, to begin with!"

The crowd laughed.

"But as it is with all those who try to obstruct the way of goodness," Sir Aleck continued, "you reap what you sow, and you only end up burning yourself in the process. Guy Fawkes, cheers."

Sir Aleck threw Guy Fawkes's effigy into the main bonfire, and it began to burn. The crowd cheered.

Darcy stood there watching the scene as Caroline Bingley, pretending to be shocked, sought solace by wrapping her arm in his.

Looking down on the letter in his pocket, Darcy tried to stay focused on what was going on around him, but it was all in vain. He knew where his mind was going to settle. He was going to Rosings Park. And he would face Elizabeth Bennet.

CHAPTER 4

FRIENDS UNTIL THE VERY END

The time before I was to go to Hunsford Parsonage with Sir William and his daughter, Maria, was now only two days away. I found, despite that the occasion was not to be a lighthearted one, I was truly finding interest and appeal in going. I was desirous to see Charlotte again, and since my father had passed and Jane had already gone with our Aunt and Uncle Gardiner to their home in London, I was open to another adventure. Any vexation that would have arisen in me from worry over how our estate was going to be run was not long to be heated, for our Uncle Phillips had indeed promised to visit Longbourn often and make sure that all was well. But with our father gone, the equilibrium of our family still felt fragile.

However, there was *one* acquaintance who I had the pleasure of seeing once more, and it did make me somewhat regret my plans for leaving the county.

Alongside Mary, Kitty and Lydia, I walked into town on the eve of my trip, with the consideration of perhaps buying some new ribbon or other ornaments that might look tastefully flattering on a bonnet.

As we were considering entering Grainley's Dress and Apparel shop, we had not reached the doorway when I felt someone's breath along my neck, and a face appear next to mine from behind.

"That ribbon in the window, I daresay, would flatter your intelligent eyes forever."

Knowing who the voice belonged to, I did not start in fear but only smiled.

"I do not know if my eyes are so very intelligent," I retorted, letting my eyes twinkle to indicate my light tone. "But rather, they are heavy as coal."

"I have never known them to be so. For they possess starlight within them."

"Mr. Wickham!" Lydia cried. "You better have a compliment for me as well."

"And I," Kitty echoed the sentiments.

Turning around, Mr. George Wickham stood there, looking as handsome as ever in his regimentals.

Behind Mr. Wickham were his friends and fellow soldiers in the regiment of—shire, Denny and Carter.

"But," Denny said, bowing to us with Mr. Wickham and Carter, "if he were to compliment you three, then where would that leave us?"

"Indeed," Carter added, "for we possess the right to be equally as gallant in our effusions of sincere flattery."

"And then we wish to put our gallantry into actions rather than them resting at words," Mr. Wickham responded, "by boldly helping you choose what ribbon you wish to flatter your already handsome features."

"You waste your flattery on us after being most abusive!" Lydia wailed.

"Lydia!" I chided her, but she did not care and only continued, as was her perpetual way to do.

"For now, we know that you are engaged to Miss King, and so you have made us all miserable as you take yourself away from bachelorhood and break our hearts."

"Well, my heart will never be broken so easily," Mary interjected. "And I care not for ribbons."

"Then why did you come, grumpy?" Lydia administered.

"She came to purchase a book," I came to Mary's defense, "which is always a respectable employment."

"Yes," Mr. Wickham replied, "it is always a useful employment."

"Indeed," Denny added, "reading! Always in favor of that."

"Now," Carter said, offering Kitty his arm, "to the ribbon!"

"To the ribbon," Kitty repeated, laughing. Denny took Lydia's arm, and the couples entered the shop. Turning to Wickham, I smiled and then saluted him.

"At ease, gentle soldier," I jested.

"Always at ease," he returned my salute, "gentle lady."

Behind us, Mary averted her eyes and entered the shop before us.

"That ribbon in the window really would look exquisite on you," he complimented me when we entered.

As vain as it would be for me to admit such a thing, but Mr. Wickham's presence was like a balm, and it softened my woes. His handsome features, his gentle manners, his elegance of speech, and the comfort he exuded made me safe in unfolding anything and everything to him.

"But should I dare think of ribbons now?" I asked him. "Do I have that right when I should still wear black? When I am still a child without a father."

"Forgive me," he responded, his expression turning more grave, "but I see that my compliments have come too soon towards yourself."

"No," I said as we entered the shop, "they came in the proper moment. I just have this sad tendency that I fear cannot be remedied."

"And what tendency is that?"

"I have a habit of seeing you and always speaking my mind, be it charming or not so charming. What should I do to remedy this?" I asked. "What prescription could there be for such a disease?"

"I would recommend, as a cure, that you only speak more with me and not less."

"But I have no choice unless I am mistaken. For, as is the announcement that all Hertfordshire knows, you shall soon have a wife, and she shall take up all your time."

When I spoke, his smile faded, and he looked down at the floor.

"Silence?" I continued, arching my eyebrow. "Oh dear, what an intimidating thing. For, give me poniards and pistols, but silence is something that I cannot face."

Mr. Wickham looked around, and he saw a bonnet against the wall.

"I say, there," he pointed, "that is a lovely bonnet. It is light and breezy. Come and let us look on it together."

Perfectly willing to obey, I walked over to the wall with him. Once getting there, I noticed that we were on the furthest sides of the wall, and no one was near us.

"Yes," I said, awkwardly, "this bonnet is lovely."

"Yes, it is."

A pause passed between us, and I thought of how to fill it when Mr. Wickham spoke first.

"Say it," he voiced.

"Say what?"

"Say that I am a villain," he elaborated, "for that is what I am."

This acknowledgment was, of course, met with surprise, but it did not silence my tongue.

"A villain?" I repeated. "Why? What sin have you committed of late? Have you run over someone with a carriage? I shall alert the designated mob that is always on the east side of Meryton, and we shall create a lynching party."

"I would deserve it," he said, his eyes firm and his tone sincere.

"Would you?" I asked, looking into his eyes.

"Yes, for I know the reason that you accost me with such affability and friendship is because of your genuinely good nature. Yet, even with such an obliging nature as yours, it cannot be denied that I have wronged you. Let us speak plainly."

We were interrupted by Lydia and Kitty, who dashed in next to us to show us the ribbons they were choosing. I complimented their styles, and then I whispered to Wickham, "We shall have no chance to privacy here. May we invite you to take tea with us? For the grounds of Longbourn are lovely at this time of year."

"Thank you," he said. "I shall inform Denny and Carter. They shall forgive my presumption at inviting them before asking them. Although I know they shall enjoy the scheme."

"I am certain they shall."

We paid for our purchases. Mary went over to the bookstore, purchased a book, and the three soldiers escorted us home where our mother met them with alacrity, eagerness and happy at being diverted.

That did not stop her from speaking of how our father's death constantly made her nervous, how forlorn we all were, and how the hallways of our home felt as if our father was still with us. These sentiments were very pretty and proper for the first couple of minutes, but she expressed her grief for too long.

After twenty minutes, we were able to disentangle Denny, Carter and Wickham from our mother's side, and we walked along the grounds. Carter and Denny knew the routine at this point. Allowing Kitty and Lydia to dominate their attention, both men escorted them to our yard, and they played horseshoes together while Wickham and I walked in the other direction.

"So," I began, "after taking many different routes, we have returned to the conversation that we began at."

"It was worth the wait," he responded, "because I wish for you to know me in full."

"You think that I am angry with you for choosing Miss King to be your wife, are you not?"

Mr. Wickham darted his eyes to the ground.

"Are you?" he asked.

"No, I am not," I assured him. When hearing this, he looked up, his expression light again.

"You are not? You do not despise me despite that I may deserve it?"

"I speak in earnest," I offered. "I do not despise you. Despite that your company is always a great pleasure to have, I choose to embrace realism and rationality. My vanity will not be allowed to take possession of me—I refuse to let it. Therefore, despite that you shall always be an acquaintance I always wish to see, I am also aware that this match you have made, in a prudential light, has all the attributes of gain. It is logical, it is sensible, and therefore, it is sound. After all, unlike my sisters, I have learned, long ago, that young and handsome men must have something to live on as well as the plain."

"It is the trappings of wealth," Mr. Wickham explained. "Perhaps, if we had been raised under a more unfortunate star, things would have been different. For, in the limited experience that I have with those in poverty, they do marry for love more often than not. They can afford it since they have no prospects. But I was not born poor, and neither were you. Both of us have been exposed to the qualities of elevated rank, and any sort of reduction would be us disobliging all those who were around us. So, you and I were born with all the qualities of two people who were suited for one another, but not the purses for it. I know I look mercenary now."

"You are being practical, which is a quality that I have no choice but to respect, for I practice it myself. Yet, do you like Miss King? Is there at least some affection in the case? I would feel more kindly toward the notion of you marrying her in consideration of her fortune, as long as you and she at least enjoy each other's company."

"Yes, she and I do get along quite well, and I do care to make her happy…in my way."

"Then, that is very well."

"It lessens the crime of my potentially being a fortune hunter, I pray. The world encourages us to marry in consideration of the income of the person that we are marrying. Then it slanders us when we do. How do we fully gain in this society?"

"Must everything be an accident of birth?"

"Truly, must it? You can only be perfect if you were wealthy from birth and maintained it. But any other lifestyle or habit is condemned or shall never be allowed to be pure in outlook and reception."

"If only we could set the pressures of the world down and never let them oppress our imaginations and choices. But the world is not going anywhere, and we must move around in it as best we may."

"Miss Bennet," he turned to me, his tone serious again, "you must believe, that if I were a man of fortune or with the ability to be a gentleman who had at least enough income to have an establishment where my wife and I could live in ease, then my choice of wife would have been a lot different than my choosing now. I would have chosen someone who was closer to my heart...I would have..."

I knew his meaning, and it weighed heavily upon me only for a moment.

My body grew still under the implications of his words. I flattered myself, but it felt as if he could only have been referring to myself.

"I also tell myself that life would have also been different if the late Mr. Darcy had never had a son," I said. "You could have been given so many gifts that would allow you to make the choice you wished. However, when I consider life, from the lofty perspective of one who might be looking down from the clouds, I see things in a wider way. If the late Mr. Darcy's son had not disobeyed his father's wishes and refused to offer you the clergyman position at Kympton Church, then you would never have come to Hertfordshire and joined the regiment. And we never would have met. I do not mean to imply that I am happy for your misfortunes, of course."

"But my misfortunes brought me here."

"So, it follows, that Mr. Darcy's actions led to us meeting one another, for if it had been the reverse, then we would have passed through life, never knowing the other."

"And that would be a bitter thing."

"Also, you never would have found your Miss King. Therefore, despite his terrible schemes and machinations, Mr. Darcy has brought you better fortune than you would have ever known."

"Then, despite myself, I have no choice but to thank him for many things."

"I would never put you so far down that you had to do that."

"No," he countered, "perhaps I must. After all, when looking back on my life, perhaps I have so much to be content over, and his actions forced me to find another life for myself. And I have no choice but to admit that being independent does suit me. Damn you, Darcy! Oh, forgive my vulgar speech there."

"Men like Mr. Darcy do sometimes lead to one professing in that way," I laughed. "I still cannot tolerate him much myself, but at last, you have your peace."

Mr. Wickham looked into my eyes, and his charm seemed more overwhelming than usual. His handsomeness was like the rays of the sun, and his manner and countenance would always spark the very best emotions within me.

In spite of this cold heart, perhaps I am—for that was the most influence he would ever have on my heart.

"If I may," he requested, taking my hand. He raised it to his lips and kissed it. "I just wished to have done that once. Did I do it well?"

"You get full marks," I professed. "No one else could have found more wanting."

Denny, Carter and Wickham took their leave, and the whole party had been perfectly cordial on both sides. I felt at peace, and my pride was not able to rest in its proper place. Mr. Wickham had preferred me above all, and I could not deny that I was truly flattered at the attentions of it.

Although I was very well contented. Despite Mr. Wickham being everything that was charming and dear to me, I was uncertain if my feelings ran as deeply as his did. I was honored by the attentions he gave me, but when first meeting him, I was at the time in my life where I didn't require a permanent attachment to anything or anyone. My days were light, my attitude cheery and all seemed possible. Therefore, why, right at the beginning of my life, did I have to resign myself to a particular fate just yet?

Ah, to be free from the shackles of any new arrangement!

That was me before my father had passed.

However, despite that my situation had changed, I still felt resolved. I would marry *if and when* I chose. Not one moment sooner… if that moment were to ever come.

Therefore, while my sisters lamented their grief of his sealed fate when the trio had left, I parted ways with Mr. Wickham in a perfectly disinterested manner.

He was near to my heart.

But he never fully had it.

And I daresay that perhaps no man ever would.

CHAPTER 5

THE AGONY OF ECSTASY

The next day brought the day of moving onward to another adventure and situation.

Sir William Lucas and his other daughter, Maria, were in his carriage with me seated next to Maria as our journey began. With all our luggage placed in the back of it, we set out for the half-day's journey it would take for us to arrive in Kent.

Sir William Lucas was a man who I had known practically all my life, and therefore, there was nothing new to contribute to the conversation. Maria was of the same situation as well, but because she had seen less of the world than her father had, she was a creature of even less information than him.

However, I never begrudged them for this because they were congenial, kind, jovial and willing to speak about the common trivialities of life that filled up our everyday actions.

At one time in my life, I may have lain a few witty criticisms at their feet for having heads full of very little within them; however, life taught me to enjoy people of that sort. Both of them were neither vicious nor mean-spirited; therefore, when a person has no harm to their character, what need is there to find fault with them? Besides, at one point in time, I discovered that sometimes being *smart* came at the price of being unpleasant. Sir William and Maria had simply chosen to be pleasant people. And since they were always apt to make themselves agreeable to everyone, there was nothing about them to fear, which was a sort of charm, in its own way.

As we sat there in the carriage, I felt disposed to make myself keener on starting the subject of discussion. I suppose, considering my desire to have a conversation originate from myself was because of two motives. First, I knew that both of them were of the sort to not chastise me being the initial one to speak and secondly, because…well, I suppose it was that my father had passed away. Sir William, who was always a kind man and my father's peer, now held a strange place in my affections. I had no father now, so, Sir William was the closest thing to a substitute when having an elderly man to converse with. He lacked my father's wit and sardonic humor, but it mattered not. My present situation left me more interested in not taking my friends for granted.

"Sir William," I asked, "I know that we have yet to see Rosings Park. However, from all that the late Mr. Collins has described of it, do you think it as large as St. James Court?"

"I believe so," Sir William responded, happily willing to talk about a subject that was the main part of his life.

I had heard about St. James Court practically all my life. It was Sir William's principal subject ever since he had been granted his knighthood there and was elevated to a higher rank where he no longer was a man of a profession. And like the rest of us in the gentry, he spent his life living at leisure and pleasure but did not always have much to speak of that was new or different than what he spoke of the day before… and the day before that. However, I was prepared for the same old of the *same old*, since it allowed the comforts of being something that I was always familiar with.

"At St. James Court," Sir William continued, "I am certain Lady Catherine de Bourgh has gone to. And if not, I believe she would be familiar with others who have been knighted there. Oh, to think! To be going to an estate which is as grand as Rosings. Do you both think she might like to hear the story of my knighthood? I do believe it would be amusing for her."

"I should think so, father," Maria offered.

"She might very well find your story diverting," I added, encouraging him, "for, if Mr. Collins had felt affection for you as his father-in-law, then he would have mentioned it to her. She very well may ask you herself. And if she does not, then Maria and I could begin to speak of the subject, and our words of it would hint for the great Lady to question what we speak of."

"I do not know if I am up for the task of speaking at all," Maria admitted fretfully. "The idea of Lady Catherine de Bourgh scares the life out of me. I do not know if I shall be able to even have a voice to speak."

"I have a bit of advice to give you," I offered. "Take it or leave it as you wish, for I give you leave to do that. Wealthy people of this sort of largeness fall on one side of a coin. The first side of the coin is the side where they are used to people being in awe of them and enjoy the idea of making people silent around them. The other side of the coin has those prestigious people who are vexed at the idea of people looking at them differently than anyone else. After two minutes of making Lady Catherine's acquaintance, we shall know which side of the coin she falls on. If she is the first side of the coin, you may be silent all that you wish. If she is the second side, then treat her as you would treat Mr. Weston, the butcher."

Sir William and Maria laughed at this.

"Wisdom indeed," Sir William complimented me. "Miss Bennet, I do recall meeting both sets of great men and ladies as that when I was presented at St. James Court. Indeed, there was one set, a family of Osbournes, and they were a mixed set. Half of them were all ease and gentility, and the other half spoke not a word to anyone else around them. I recall every single aspect of them. And then there was this other family, the Eliots, and they were also such an amusing sort."

Sir William continued to speak of every particular person that he had met at St. James Court. Eventually, the subject was exhausted, and after similar subjects were dropped, I looked out the window and gazed at the scenery we passed by.

This was peace.

Only for me to later discover that this was one of the many moments of the calm before the storm.

And to Hunsford Parsonage, we arrived!

Since our arrival was less than a quarter of an hour later than we had planned, Charlotte was already waiting for us. Having spied our carriage from a window, she rushed out to meet us.

Upon our carriage stopping, Sir William stepped down and offered his hand to Maria and me, helping us out of it gracefully.

"Charlotte, I am so sorry!" Maria said, embracing her older sister. "Oh, my dear, my dear!"

Charlotte laughed sadly as she embraced her sister as well.

"You came, and so I am the better for it," Charlotte responded, then her father patted her cheek.

"Oh, my unfortunate daughter," Sir William offered.

"Father, do not call me unfortunate, or I do not believe that I shall be able to support myself," Charlotte responded.

"Nonsense," I interjected, "supporting yourself is something that you excel at."

Sir William and Maria stepped aside, and I got a glimpse of my old friend in full.

Charlotte Lucas.

Charlotte Collins.

Now Widow Collins.

Walking up to her, Charlotte and I took hands.

We were happy to see each other again.

Soon after warm words were spoken, we entered Hunsford Parsonage. Charlotte arranged for tea, and we were given refreshments.

Now feeling among friends, Charlotte did not stand on ceremony. Assuming that we would be tired from our journey, she did not give us a tour of the grounds or the whole parsonage, but rather, she allowed us to retire to our rooms, getting a bit of rest till suppertime.

"After all," she announced when we accepted this scheme, "making you tour a home will not change the state that my life is already in. Let conversation fall where it may, especially when it has all the time in the world to do so."

That was Charlotte Lucas, practical until the very end.

When I went to my room, I had begun to unpack my things when Charlotte entered with some chocolate.

"I thank you," I said, as I got done placing my gowns on the shelves. Ceasing my unpacking, I took the chocolate and began to drink it. "This is delicious."

"I knew that you all would enjoy it. Lizzy, it really is delightful to see you again."

"And I, you. Charlotte, I am sorry for your loss," I began. "I know that I have said it in my letter, but now I get to say it directly."

"Thank you for your condolences," Charlotte responded. "But in truth, I see what you are feeling."

"And what am I feeling?"

"Perhaps as if life has given me what I deserved for what I did."

"You think I am happy for your misfortune?"

"No, I know you are not vindictive in that manner. But I also know you find pleasure in seeing life give everyone the result to their own actions. Lizzy, when I had married Mr. Collins, it was not to wound you or to marry the man who would inherit your father's estate."

"I know now," I allowed. "I confess that I felt pain at your choice initially, as you well know. Yet time taught me that you did what you chose to do because you viewed it as one of your very last chances to make up your life. But yes, I will not deny that I was… angry for a time."

"And your anger is now put to rest as well as your mother's worries perhaps on my side. For as you can see, I have not even been married for little over half a year, and I am not with child."

"You are not?" I asked, with one eyebrow. Sighing, she sat on the bed next to me.

"No, I am not."

"Are you certain?"

"Yes, I am certain. My poor Mr. Collins passed away without a line following him. So, his side of the family name will die."

"You do not presume to look on yourself as a failure for it, do you?"

"I cannot control how fate works. Or rather, I cannot control how fate deals me a blow in the name of justice. I married a man who would inherit my friend's home, and he dies before I can even fully enjoy the benefits of marriage and the comfort of a child. Therefore, I cannot help but accept that perhaps, fate does have at most a sense of humor or at least a scale in which she weighs justice being executed. She was perhaps simply waiting for the right time to strike and bring her gavel crashing down upon me. You cannot deny that you have had this thought as well?"

I bit my lip.

"Very well," I confessed. "I did feel this way for some time."

"I do not despise you for the feeling. And nor do I despise your mother for feeling as if I have gotten what I deserved."

"My mother does not speak of it very often."

"That is a lie," she chuckled.

"No, it is not."

"Yes, it is."

"Oh, very well, it is."

"What has she said about it all?"

"You do not want to know."

"You may tell me."

"Truly, you do not wish to know."

"No, you may tell me."

"She said, 'Mr. Collins is dead. Mrs. Collins gets nothing, and all is right in the world.'"

"Oh," Charlotte said, "yes, that does sound like her."

We both gave each other a look, and then we laughed gently.

"Well, you can all now set your hearts at rest," Charlotte said while she helped me unpack my belongings. "I am no longer a threat at all. And I never desired to be a threat, to begin with. I just wanted to..."

"Yes?"

"I no longer wished to be a burden on my parents," she finished. "I am almost thirty, Lizzy. This was my last chance. And now it shall forever be this way."

"You know that I do not possess your sentiments," I acknowledged. "But, as far as differences of situation and temper lay, your views were sound. Take comfort then, for you did your duty. Everything else was out of your hands. But, if this question is not something you wish to consider, then you need not answer it—but what about your heart? How are your emotions affected by such a loss?"

"They are what they are, I suppose."

"That is a very indirect and general answer. Therefore, I can only assume that you do not desire to answer it."

"I do not answer it because I am ashamed."

"In what manner?"

"I felt agony when Mr. Collins passed away, and I mourned him…somewhat. But Lizzy, despite that he did possess kindness, in his own way, as well as consideration for my comforts—I could not cry. I wanted desperately to cry. Even at his funeral service, I did all in my power to force the emotion to arrive. I said, 'Charlotte, cry now. You must weep.' Yet, I could not do it. I felt all the insensitivity of my actions."

Empathetic, I draped my arm around her shoulder, she rested her head on my shoulder blade, and she let out her grief—the grief of someone who was feeling guilt about not feeling any worse.

"And whatever tears I shed now," she continued, "will be all from a selfish motive. I feel foolish, lost and without shelter."

"You have family, you have friends, and you have Lucas Lodge. And your emotions right now do not have to be distant, disinterested or even pretty. There is no reason to stand on ceremony, for there is no one here to judge you. Feel what you feel, or else it will only consume you."

"Thank you."

"I would have come a lot sooner than now. Well, of course you know this, since we were meant to visit months ago, but as you know, tragedy struck my life around that time as well."

"I am being selfish again. I have not asked you about your father."

"We wrote to each other enough for me to know your condolences by heart."

"I am sorry. He was a good man, Lizzy, and he loved you terribly."

"And I loved him. We both have lost the men who have

sheltered us, and therefore, what remains is for us to decide what happens now?"

"Yes."

We both looked at the wall, staring ahead at the blankness of it. I do believe, in that one second, the wall matched our concept of the future. For a brief moment, we did not know where to go… or what was to come next.

I knew, with fortitude and temperance, that I could weather such ignorance and doubt. In time, Charlotte would, as well.

"So," Charlotte said, as we finished unpacking and began to head downstairs for supper. "Now that Longbourn is safe from going to us Collins' family, what will become of it? Will you all finally get to keep the home?"

"The law shall naturally see to it that it is handed down to the next appropriate male who seems the most likely to be worthy of it. Our Uncle Phillips is sorting out all the legal technicalities that go along with such complicated matters. He is seeing if Longbourn can be passed down to my Uncle Gardiner, for, after all, he is my mother's brother and the best candidate for it."

"Your Uncle Phillips is a good man. I am certain that he shall do his best."

"Oh, to have an attorney in the family!" I remarked. "For once, being a family of profession has worked in our favor!"

Sir William and Maria joined us at the dinner table, and we all sat down to eat. I do believe, despite the sadness that lay on both sides, we really did come close to that thing called happiness.

CHAPTER 6

*T*he next day after breakfast, Charlotte had been showing us the grounds around Hunsford when suddenly a phaeton drew up to the front of the parsonage.

"Who is that?" Maria asked.

"That is Miss Anne de Bourgh," Charlotte said. "She must be coming to pay her respects. Excuse me, I shall introduce you all presently."

Charlotte approached the phaeton, and I got my first glimpse of Miss Anne de Bourgh herself. She was a woman whose reputation preceded her, and I learned of her existence long before she would ever know of mine. Long had I heard of her prestigious manners and regal countenance from Mr. Collins, and long had I decided to not believe a word that he said whenever he spoke of the de Bourgh family. His perspective, I had gathered, naturally came from a place of prejudice and favoritism…and I was proven to be absolutely correct. From the angle that we saw her, Miss Anne de Bourgh looked pale, thin, out of spirits and a little sickly. In short, from the perspective of appearances, she had very little to recommend her.

"Oh, my goodness, Lizzy and Papa," Maria whispered to us. "That is Miss Anne de Bourgh! Can you believe it? I would scarce believe it myself if she were not right before our eyes." She stepped forward and then twirled around suddenly. "Did you see? She just turned around and looked at us. Miss de Bourgh looked at *us!*"

"Indeed, I believe she did," Sir William whispered in response. "Maria and Lizzy, I daresay that you shall become favorites very quickly."

"Only if she regards strangers as charming," I responded. "If so, then we stand a chance."

Charlotte turned to us and gestured for us to come towards them. We were going to meet the woman who I had heard much about.

As we approached the phaeton, I heard Mr. Wickham's words return to my memory. When he had discovered that my cousin, Mr. Collins, was the reverend at Hunsford Parsonage, it was him who informed me of a deeper connection.

'It is curious that Mr. Collins should mention Lady Catherine de Bourgh,' he informed me, *'and quite the coincidence. Lady Catherine de Bourgh is Mr. Darcy's aunt, and her daughter, Miss Anne de Bourgh, is destined to be Mr. Darcy's bride.'*

'Really?' I responded, and then I added, most amused, *'Poor Miss Bingley'.*

And now poor Miss Bingley indeed! Here I was, walking towards the woman who was actually destined to marry Mr. Darcy. Before now, I was the woman who was there to witness Miss Bingley do everything in her power to attract Mr. Darcy toward herself. All her schemes, all of her plans and machinations, and they were all for nothing! Truly, it was much ado about nothing in the end. How deliciously comical. Miss Caroline Bingley had never been my friend, nor even a comfortable acquaintance, but rather a strain and a pain to be near. As a result, to know that she would reap no rewards for her efforts at winning Mr. Darcy's heart was the perfect sort of revenge for me. How often it was that a person did not need to seek vengeance themselves. For people often exposed themselves to their own punishment, and Miss Bingley was one of those individuals.

We approached Miss de Bourgh and curtsied and bowed. It turned out that the woman who was with her was Mrs. Jenkinson, who attended the young lady. Soon into the acquaintance, Miss de Bourgh's character became easy to uncover, discover and determine. She was a young woman whose wealth had done little to save. Or rather, it could not save. She had no conversation, no particular skills at drawing comfort from those around her. She seemed to not care about our existence one way or the other and was simply going through motions. It was Charlotte who often asked her questions and got very concise answers in return. The sentence, *I shall ask mother to see if she will request your company's presence at Rosings,* was the longest answer that she gave to us before she was off to return home.

"What do you think of her?" Charlotte asked me as we walked into the house.

"My thoughts are not the most congenial," I admitted. "But I shall say this, she looks spiritless and cross. She will do for him nicely, and she shall make him a proper wife."

"Who?"

"Mr. Darcy. She's destined to be his bride."

Charlotte's eyes widened at this.

"No, that cannot be," Charlotte whispered.

"But it is," I responded, and I could feel my eyes twinkle. "When it comes to two people who are all dourness and above being pleased, they shall be perfectly matched. This is their destiny, but he seems to be the sort to walk into it freely. I welcome this, for he shall end his single life the way that he began our acquaintance —out of spirits."

We entered the house again.

A year ago…

All over Hertfordshire, there had been news of a single man of vast fortune coming into our neighborhood, and he went by the name of Bingley. But what sparked everyone even more was the next report that spread around the village. The rumor declared that he came with a large party, and the chief among the company was a man by the name of Mr. Fitzwilliam Darcy of Pemberly, who was to inherit ten thousand pounds a year. This income rendered him handsome, even before being seen, but his handsome appearance was soon to be displayed to all when the Netherfield party was to come to our ball at the assembly room.

They did, and their party consisted of the two aforementioned men, Miss Bingley, Mrs. Hurst and her husband—who I always forget exists because he does nothing to make you remember him.

Mr. Bingley did everything in his power to make himself agreeable to everyone in the room, and he succeeded. He danced every dance and danced twice with Jane. This marked attention strengthened Jane's reputation of being the greatest of us Bennet sisters. While Mr. Bingley impressed all, Mr. Darcy offended all.

Mr. Darcy stood up with no other women but the women in his company, looked annoyed if anyone dared speak to him, and was constantly giving offense.

However, his particular slight towards myself was perhaps the most alarming, for not only did he refuse to stand up with me when my mother offered my hand as a dancing partner, I overheard him speaking with his friend about their time at the dance.

'*Come, Darcy,*' Mr. Bingley had entreated his taciturn friend. '*You had much better dance. I hate to see you standing about in this stupid manner. Come, I must have you dance.*'

'*I shall not,*' Mr. Darcy had replied. '*In an assembly such as this, it would be unsupportable. Your sisters are engaged at present, and you know that it will be a pain for me to stand up with another woman.*'

'*Good god, Darcy! I would not be so fastidious as you are for a kingdom. I have never seen such lovely manners and pleasant company in my life, and some of the women here are uncommonly pretty.*'

Mr. Bingley cast his eye upon my sister, for he had been referring to her. Mr. Darcy had caught his eye and also looked on my sister.

'*You have been dancing with the only handsome woman in the room,*' Mr. Darcy admitted.

'*Darcy, she is the most beautiful creature that I ever beheld. Yet, look more to your right, and you shall see her sister. Elizabeth is her name, I believe. She is very pretty too, and I daresay very agreeable. Let me have her sister introduce you so that you may feel more comfortable standing up with her for a dance.*'

'*Who?*'

Mr. Darcy turned and looked on me. Here, I had the presence of mind to have been looking away when they had been speaking about me. Therefore, I remained looking aloof while still noting them from the side of my vision. I had seen Mr. Darcy's eyes fall on me, and then look away sharply.

'Do not attempt it, Bingley, nor force me to suffer the slings and arrows of being forced to endure a dance that would put pain to us both. Besides, she is tolerable, I suppose. Although she is not handsome enough to tempt me.'

'You quibble, Darcy.'

'My quibbles are to the purpose and to the proper point. Bingley, I am in no mood to entertain ladies who have been slighted by other men. She sits down, and no other man shall stand up with her. Therefore, I am under no obligations to save anyone in this matter. You may return to your partner and enjoy her smiles—her many smiles. You are wasting your time with me.'

'You win this round, for now,' Bingley had relented and returned to Jane…

And that was the first night that I had met Mr. Darcy. Yes, Miss Anne de Bourgh would make him a proper wife, indeed!

———

"Lizzy!"

It had been merely a few hours since Miss de Bourgh's departure when I heard my name being called. The crier turned out to be Maria, who rushed into my room.

"Lizzy, what do you think?" She laughed. "We have been invited to dine at Rosings Park tomorrow afternoon!"

"Have we?" I asked.

"Yes," she declared, grabbing my hand and pulling me out of the room. "Charlotte shall read you the letter."

I allowed her to drag me down the steps, where indeed, Charlotte had a letter, and it was an invitation to dine at Rosings Park.

"Now that is generosity at its best!" Sir William declared. "To invite us so soon after our arrival. Is it not so, Lizzy?"

"Yes," I responded, "so it would seem."

"This may very well be a compliment to you all coming," Charlotte said.

"I believe so," her father augmented. "I believe so. Such condescension I have never seen, except for when I was presented at St. James's Court. There was this one time where…"

Once more, he began to recall an anecdote from his day of knighthood. We all sat and waited for him to finish, which, fortunately, was not very long.

———

The next day arrived, and we soon made our way to Rosings Park. As we did so, I was able to admire the grounds, somewhat, for the little bit that I had seen was overall quite lovely. Some areas looked rather contrived as opposed to natural, but that was the fashion of the times. Our gardeners did all in their power to present nature at its best by tailoring everything to fit a pre-designed look. Although, sometimes the synthesis of nature and pretense do not always coincide, and that could be seen with certain aspects of Rosings Park. It was lovely, to be sure, but sometimes, it seemed like it was trying too hard.

Then we came in view of the house.

And it was a beautiful and great home, to be sure. I marveled at it. We all honestly labeled it as a handsome building, but I was saving my interest for the characters we would meet within. *They* were what I had come to see.

We entered the stately home and were immediately impressed with the interior—then came the great moment. We waited patiently, and then we were presented to Lady Catherine de Bourgh herself. Her daughter was sitting next to her with Mrs. Jenkinson tending to her.

Now came the moment of truth.

Mr. Collins had informed us that Lady Catherine de Bourgh had been the most affable and excellent woman he had ever met.

Mr. Wickham had warned me that this was not so and that she could be an insufferably proud woman.

Now came the moment of truth.

We all curtsied to her while Sir William bowed. Also, he and Maria, if I was not mistaken, had a very distraught look on their faces. They were scared out of their wits!

"So," Lady Catherine greeted, "this is your father, Sir William, and your younger sister, Miss Maria."

"Yes, your ladyship," Charlotte responded.

"And this is Miss Elizabeth Bennet, who was the late Mr. Collins's cousin."

"I am, your ladyship," I said. This sudden speaking out of turn clearly had a marked impression upon the great lady.

"Well, you must be saddened over your cousin's passing," she announced. "Yet, I do not doubt if there is also a bit of relief. For I understand that he was to inherit Longbourn."

"I often do not allow the words 'relief' and 'passing' to be felt within the same sentence," I administered. "although while I do feel relief over my home still belonging to my mother and sisters at present, I never felt its remaining with us as higher than valuing the life of my cousin. Therefore, I suppose, in your eyes, my feelings are a little complicated."

"You speak much for a person who has just been introduced."

"I thought you were no less deserving than a true answer."

Lady Catherine looked me up and down.

"You may all sit."

We all sat down.

"Mrs. Collins," Lady Catherine said, "your friend here seems to be a pretty and genteel sort of girl."

"I thank you, your ladyship," I said.

"But looks mean nothing if you are not accomplished. I shall inquire about your accomplishments in a moment to value your worth."

My worth! What a thing to say!

"Now," Lady Catherine continued, "Mrs. Collins, as I said before, I am sorry for your sake that Longbourn shall never go to you. But if my advice had been listened with apt attention, then you would not be in this predicament. For I advised you and Mr. Collins to produce an heir as quickly as may be, and you did not obey my advice. Now, you are experiencing the effects of not heeding my counsel, and you and he have no one to answer for it but yourselves."

My eyebrows raised at this. Surely the woman could not have sped up their attempts of having a child.

"However," Lady Catherine continued, now turning to me, "your predicament also originates from individuals such as myself not being consulted. Your estate was entailed to the male line, of course, for that is how Mr. Collins was to inherit it."

"Yes, it—"

"Well, if I had been there when that arrangement had begun, then there would have been no need to worry over such matters. The de Bourgh family never believed in male primogeniture, and a wiser notion has never occurred before. Truly, if I had been there, then Longbourn would never have required a son for it to be passed down to."

"Your ladyship's will would have been nice to bestow upon our home," I admitted. "For any child not to inherit their parents' estate shall never make a great deal of sense, especially regarding that women and men are equally up to the task of anything."

"I did not say that, for there are some things young ladies ought not to do which men, of course, have the province."

"Such as? I have never encountered any situation where we could not do what a gentleman could."

Lady Catherine's eyebrows raised.

"You give your opinion very decidedly for so young a person. It borders on rash boldness."

"I speak as I find. I have never seen anything that we are not up to the task for."

"I admire your confidence in our abilities, but what of war? Surely, you cannot believe a woman able to undertake such a task as soldiering?"

"I can believe so because we already have. There have been female warriors in history."

"Those cultures were mostly savage and lacked refinement of true society."

"Joan of Arc was a formidable warrior."

"She was French. I rest my case."

"France may be our old enemy, but I cannot believe that they are barbaric. There can still be honor amongst enemies."

"You speak your words very boldly. Pray, what is your age?"

"With a woman such as myself, with three younger sisters—four, if you include one that died at birth, then your ladyship can hardly expect me to own to it."

"Miss Elizabeth, you cannot be more than twenty. Therefore, there is no need for you to conceal your age."

"I am not six and twenty."

When hearing that I was most likely twenty-five years old, Lady Catherine's eyebrows raised. I had not given her a direct answer, which naturally would be a great blow to her sensibilities. However, being late in years and unmarried was also probably overwhelming to her. By her calculation, and by perhaps the calculation of the world, I was an old maid. In faith, I was not afraid of the label, as Charlotte had been. And my lack of shame in the matter was perhaps another surprise to her.

Lady Catherine de Bourgh had a regality to her that displayed a woman who perhaps was handsome when she was young. But she was now a mother to a grown child, and therefore, she no longer had any pretensions of beauty. She only had the shadows of it. Her manner and air were stately, her countenance formidable and she was intimidating.

However, I was not in the mood to be intimidated.

Her hair was thin, her face had a comical heaviness to it, but perhaps, that heaviness was augmented by her very manner. Lady Catherine was impertinent at times, while also being intrusive in her questions. She was a woman who ruled the world around her, and therefore, she had nothing else to do but to rule everyone who entered the sphere that she controlled. And I, being in Rosings Park, was now within the realm of her power.

As we began to sit down to a midday meal, she continued to ask us a series of questions, but most often, she did not wait for answers. Usually, she spoke by way of command rather than in mere conversation. Very quickly, I gathered that she was a woman who loved to speak but seldom required an answer.

In truth, when I looked upon her, I saw a wealthy and more powerful version of my mother. Both women spoke with authority on every subject, whether they were experts of the subject or not, and they went mad if things did not go their way.

If Mr. Darcy chose not to marry Anne, after all, I would be surprised if Lady Catherine did not give him the same lecture that my mother had given me when I turned down Mr. Collins's offer of marriage.

Soon after our meal, I expressed a desire to be shown around the grounds of Rosings Park, and Lady Catherine was surprised at my request.

"Do you always ask for particular tours when you go to someone's home?" Lady Catherine asked me. I opened my mouth, but she continued speaking before I could continue. "While your request is forward, I can very well comprehend your desire to see my grounds. The land of Rosings Park must be infinitely superior to anything that you are accustomed to. Therefore, your eagerness shows your desire to witness superior landscape."

"Perhaps so, madame," I allowed. "In truth, I am very fond of walking."

"And you shall notice that you can walk through nothing better. My gardener's name is Tate. One of my servants shall take you to him, and you may enjoy the walk about. When you return, if you like, you may remain for dinner. I have some guests who shall attend, and they may perhaps enjoy the variety of company."

"We look forward to meeting them," Charlotte said. "Yes, father?"

Charlotte's direct question at him had alarmed Sir William. Like his younger daughter, Sir William had been struck dumb by meeting Lady Catherine and had not spoken a word since they arrived. He mumbled incoherently for a few seconds, but Lady Catherine spoke over him.

Soon, a servant came, and he escorted us out of the house and to Mr. Tate, the gardener.

I breathed a sigh of relief. I was ever so glad to be out of doors and away from the scrutinizing eyes of Lady Catherine and the awkward silence that her daughter loved to generate around herself.

When we entered the gardens being shown around by Mr. Tate, Sir William and Maria remarked on how lovely everything was. Usually, my compliments were saved for the end. Now that we were no longer in Lady Catherine's company, Sir William and his daughter got their voices back.

"So," Charlotte whispered to me, "how do you like Lady Catherine's home, Lizzy?"

"It's lovely," I allowed. "It's a very handsome home, and I can imagine why Mr. Collins was perpetually in awe of it."

"Yes, he walked to Rosings Park nearly every day."

"So often? Was that necessary?"

"Perhaps not. But I confessed that I encouraged him in that."

I suppressed a smile.

"Well, he must have always spoken to you of what occurred at Rosings when he returned back to the parsonage."

"Often, he was in his garden, tending to it, as well as his beehives, which I also encouraged him to do as often as he could. And when he wasn't there, he was often in his study."

"Between the exercise and the tending to his work, he did well to make his schedule filled."

"Yes. So, it often was that a whole day past and he and I did not spend more than a few minutes in each other's company."

"Were you able to bear the isolation cheerfully?" I guessed.

"Very cheerfully."

I very well understood her meaning. *Ah,* I thought, *to be in a marriage that was not much worth the earning!*

As we walked along, I was able to enjoy the grounds and landscape that was around Rosings Park. Mr. Tate did us a good service, and every word he spoke of the gardens was filled with well-placed pride, for he spoke clearly about the way everything was laid out to advantage. Lady Catherine's taste would always be a bit pretentious for my liking, but I could never deny that handsome *was* as handsome *was* there.

We walked down another lane, and then it opened up to a series of trees that were tall and well-shaped. Running my hands along one tree trunk, I began to lose myself among this new land that I found myself having to be washed up along.

I was there, and I was content for a brief moment. I could not explain why I felt an elation that was sparked by everything around me, but I was at the time in my life where I suppose that when a happy moment began, I desired to cling to it immediately.

Life would find me again if it had gotten away from me, to begin with. My father was gone. Longbourn was still in a state where we did not know if it belonged to us or not. My future was a blank wall, not adorned with any particular object. Although, for the moment, I would release all anxiety on that score, I would pretend that my father was still there in his study, merely waiting for me to return, and all was well.

Therefore, I wandered around the gardens, and before I knew it, I was separated from the rest of the group. This separation did not disturb or alarm me, for if I ever were to become removed from the company for too long, I could always return to the house and wait for them to return.

Onward I went, wandering through the pretty sort of wilderness that bordered one part of the estate.

In this way, I was allowed the pleasures of being alone and being free from everything.

Raising out my arms, I began to twirl around.

"To be as a bird among the wind!" I called. "To be swept away and then to go anywhere and everywhere!"

Suddenly, I heard the sound of a horse galloping from another direction. When I did, I was startled. Releasing myself from my revelry, I moved among the trees and bushes, desiring to know where the sound of the horse was coming from.

It was strange, for, due to the sound echoing in an unnatural way, it seemed as if the horse was coming from all directions.

But, the sound of its hooves became more distinct, and I was able to deduce where it was coming from.

I moved around a set of trees, and then I came right in the way of its progress.

My sudden appearance startled the creature. It reared up on its hind legs while the rider tried to regain control.

Any second, I felt that it was going to crash down upon me, crushing me to death.

Instinctively, I raced backward, trying to keep from being trampled over. However, the horse was smart, in regards to myself, but not so much in regards to its owner.

The horse did rear up on its hind legs but did not fall backward. However, as it jumped back, it swirled around on its back legs, disorientating the rider. His back was knocked up against a nearby tree forcing him to lose his grip and fall to the ground.

Fortunately, the horse did not trample over its master as it lowered its front feet on the ground, but rather made sure that it landed to the side of the man.

"By God!" I roared, rushing to the man. "I am coming, sir!"

I leaned down over him, and the desire to be of use was more than the desire to maintain propriety. I wrapped my arms around his body to roll him over and see if he was conscious.

He was alive, awake, and when he turned to me, his eyes widened upon the familiarity that we both shared with each other.

"Mr. Darcy!" I gasped.

"Miss Bennet!" he responded.

There Mr. Darcy was, on the ground and fallen, because of me.

The surprise alarmed us both.

I stared into his eyes.

He stared into mine.

In the work of a few seconds, it felt as if we were locked within an eternity. Our eyes, unblinking and fixed on the shock of seeing each other again in such a way, left us both overwhelmed and forgetting the situation that we were in.

Silence reigned, and our confusion reigned alongside it.

Next, his horse made a neighing sound, and it woke us both from our frozen state.

"Miss Bennet," he repeated, then, to my utter surprise, he raised his hand to my cheek and placed his palm and fingers along my face. This brief touch surprised me for only a second before his next question followed. "Are you injured? Did I hurt you at all?"

"No, I am unharmed," I assured him. "Your horse was wise. He stopped immediately and did not fall at all upon me. But his wisdom did not produce the best results for you, I see. How are you, sir? Are you hurt?"

"I am not certain. With falls such as these, sometimes injuries produce themselves immediately, and other times, they produce themselves on the very next day. Time will tell."

"But until then, we can't let you sleep here, now can we?" I asked. "Your aunt would never let me hear the end of it. Do you need help standing up?"

"I do not think so."

Mr. Darcy tried to rise, but when he placed pressure on his right hand, he collapsed again.

"Your wrist?" I asked.

"I believe that I fell wrong on it," he said. "It is painful."

"Then it would do best not to put any pressure on it. What about your left arm? Does that hurt at all?"

"No, it is well."

"Then I'll place myself on your other side so you can lean on your left arm to rise up. As I do, lean on me at the same time. And do not worry about me falling down. I may not be an ox, but I am a Bennet—fragile I am not. Some slight weight on me is a pressure I can bear."

Mr. Darcy leaned on his left arm, and with my help, he stood up.

"I can do well from here," he said, beginning to release me.

"You should not walk along just now," I demanded, "for you do not know if your legs are fully unharmed. Let me support you briefly, and do not mount your horse again. We should walk him to the stables."

"I can walk perfectly..." he began, but then he looked into my eyes and trailed off. I can only assume there was something about my staring at him that unnerved him, forcing him to relent. Instead, his tone and countenance changed, and I felt the weight upon me grow heavier as he accepted that I was the best support for him at that time. "Very well. Would you be so kind as to help me get to my horse?" he asked.

"Of course," I allowed. I held onto his waist as he had one of his arms draped over my shoulder. Together, we walked to his horse.

"You should be careful when you walk," he advised me, and I took the full meaning of his words. Here I was, assisting him, and he thought that it was correct to chastise me for simply walking. Mr. Darcy would always be as he was, I supposed!

"Do not dare advise or reprimand me for walking, sir," I countered, still helping him to his horse. "You know that such advice will be ill-judged, ungrateful and incongruous."

"I did not speak from a place of admonishment," he retorted, "and I gather the feeling, by the heat in your voice, that you are about to willfully misunderstand me."

"You did label me as such once, in a particular drawing room. I suppose that I am about to receive your usual tone of appreciation—which would really be a propensity to find fault somewhere."

"Is that what you believe me to be doing?" he asked, taking the reins of his horse in his left hand.

"I believe that you may."

"Then, you do misunderstand me."

"Do I?"

"Yes." He looked into my eyes, and I saw the familiar stern gaze, but within his eyes was a depth that felt as if it belonged to some other emotion. "I was saying that because I want you to take care. Imagine if my horse had trampled you. I would have never been able to forgive myself if something happened to you, and I was the means of causing that calamity."

This response alarmed me.

"Mr. Darcy, unless I am mistaken, I detect a sense of an apology in what you say. Is this your way of apologizing for almost riding over me?"

Mr. Darcy looked ahead. I was not afraid of him now, just as I had never been afraid of him before.

"Go on, Mr. Darcy," I continued, "I await your apology. Especially when your apologies are so rarely given."

"My apologies are rarely given, aren't they?"

"Yes, they are. But, if it helps, your apologies are so rarely bestowed that, if I desired your good opinion, then that would make them more worth the earning."

"Do you desire my opinion?"

I thought to say something ambiguous in tone and temperament for the sake of being respectful. However, I was not in the mood for such false pleasantries. "Not a jot," I responded, with my eyes twinkling in delight of being frank with him. "Yet take heart. For how much do I hold in esteem?"

He only stared at me again, and I knew not what else to say. Suddenly, I felt an awkwardness, and I realized the perversity of our meeting in such a manner.

"And I believe that you have to return your horse to your aunt's stables. And I have to find my friends."

"You would leave me?" he asked, and his question was so very surprising! What did he mean by asking such a thing?

"I must. Why do you sound as if I should stay? Do you plan on falling down again and hurting your other wrist?"

"I plan on knowing that you are returned to my aunt's home safely."

"I doubt that I shall be run over by a galloping rider from here to there. Besides, my friends shall be looking for me."

"Very well. Be careful, Miss Bennet."

"Be hopeful, Mr. Darcy."

I curtsied to him, and then I began to walk quickly away. As I did, I turned, took one last look at him again and saw that he was staring at me as he led his horse away.

Reality had rushed back to me at Rosings Park!

I had seen Mr. Darcy again. But due to the circumstances at the time where a calamity had united us, neither he nor I had the time to feel apprehension. Everything happened so very suddenly that all Mr. Darcy and I had time to do was to react to our crashing into one another.

There was no time to recall that I despised him.

There was not the space for him to bring forth his feelings of hatred for me.

All there was to do was to assist, on my side, and to be assisted, on his side.

However, now that we had finished crashing into each other, I was able to recall our previous history, our many moments of finding the other unbearable to be in each other's company, and for us both to be giving offense to the other. My displays of resentment for him were justifiable, for they originated from him, showing a blatant contempt for me.

All those feelings and memories were now flooding back into my mind, and now that I had time to reflect on our history, I could return back to our original way of being with each other—with vexation on my side, and cold pride on his.

However, he had held my face when he saw me again. Or did I imagine that? No, for I know that it was not just a trick of my imagination. He had broken decorum in every conceivable manner and held my face. So inappropriate!

And I had done nothing to prevent it or chastise him for forgetting himself. Why would he have committed himself to such a gesture if he still hated me?

Then I recalled that he was recovering from being in pain and having undergone a shock. Perhaps he was simply not himself. Or perhaps his feelings of animosity toward me had lessened since we had last encountered. There was a change, and it had occurred somewhere.

In that moment, I scarce knew what to think, but when I saw him next, I thought it wise to let his actions be my guide. I need not worry of how to proceed at present. Yes, that was the answer to everything.

For the present, I had one mission—find my company.

Soon, I succeeded at this, and they all had questioned me on where I was and why did I break away from them. I answered all their questions evenly and put their minds at peace. I then apologized, and everything resumed as it was.

Except for the fact that despite myself, my mind still wandered over to Mr. Darcy.

Once more, he performed the painful habit of resting in the forefront of my thoughts—and I hated him for it!

Soon, we returned back to the house, and Lady Catherine's disposition had altered somewhat. I could only suppose that it was because her nephew had come, and therefore, she had company now who she actually felt an emotional attachment to.

We were informed that since Mr. Fitzwilliam Darcy had arrived, there was a slight impediment. He had been met with an accident on the road, his hand was injured, and therefore, it was best for us to return to Hunsford Parsonage, where we were assured we would be invited again very soon.

We all agreed to this and returned to the parsonage soon after.

Along the walk home, I attempted to not think of Mr. Darcy.

When we returned, removing our outerwear, I still continued to attempt to not think of him.

When we all went to our separate rooms, where the servants had already prepared fires for us, I tried not to think of him as I undressed and placed my night garments on.

Unfortunately, of course, I thought of him.

What must he think in seeing me?

It was most inconvenient for us both to reunite in this way. But it was so.

Sitting down, I began to compose a letter to Jane, where I detailed all the events that had occurred so far. At the end, I specifically appraised her of news that she ought to deliver to mama. I said, in the most sanguine words I could, Charlotte had indeed not been with child. Therefore, Longbourn was safe from being given to a male infant that she may have produced. For Charlotte had exited her marriage in the same manner she had entered it—singular in number.

CHAPTER 7

DISTURBANCES OF COMPOSURE

When Mr. Darcy had entered Rosings Park, and Lady Catherine was immediately informed that one of her favorite nephews had entered her home wounded, it gathered all the compassion a woman like Lady Catherine could bestow. She felt empathetic for his pain, calling for the doctor in the village to come immediately, and then when discovering the means through which he harmed himself, she reprimanded him.

"Fitzwilliam," she chided him as some servants began to place a cold compress on his right wrist, "my dear boy, you truly brought this situation upon yourself. And it serves you right for making me ever so anxious about you. Rather than riding along like a country rogue everywhere, you should have arrived in a chaise and four."

"Aunt Catherine, what is lacking in etiquette by being a country rogue when I am, indeed, in the country?"

"You know very well that I am right," she continued, "for I am extremely correct in situations like these. And what do you mean, sir, by arriving without your cousin? If you had done the correct thing of arriving with him, then you would have been safely stored in a carriage, and this accident would never have occurred. Anne, are we not excessively worried about him?"

Anne was sitting on the sofa, near where this scene took place. Mrs. Jenkinson was sitting next to her.

"Yes, Mama," Anne said, her tone flat and leading the effect of her sounding like a parrot, "we are worried about him."

"How do you do, Anne?" Mr. Darcy asked. "You are looking well."

"My daughter always looks well, does she not?" Lady Catherine boasted. "You are doing splendidly, are you not, Anne?"

"Yes, I am doing splendidly," Anne confirmed.

"And are you not happy to see your dear cousin?"

"I am. Very happy."

Darcy did not speak anything after this. His relationship with Anne was, and always would be, the most painfully awkward and dull thing to endure. And to think that his aunt believed that they would make a good match!

"My journey on horseback was appropriate, I can assure you, Aunt," Darcy continued. "Richard was not able to be spared from his duties as soon as he expected. Therefore, he informed me to ride on ahead, to arrive on the planned day, and he would join us in three days' time. Therefore, you must forgive my mode of travel and praise it. It was done as the proper duty to bring you the news as soon as possible."

"I remain standing by my advice," Lady Catherine stated, "but I thank you, for it shows your ongoing attachment to Rosings and duty to your family. This shall be a fine quality when a certain desirable event is to take place here."

Lady Catherine looked between Anne and Mr. Darcy. He, nor Anne, looked at each other during this. But rather, they both said nothing and looked at the floor. This discomfort was too much of a pressure for them to bear.

Due to his accident, Darcy discovered that Lady Catherine had sent home the Hunsford company, and he was deeply undecided about his feeling for this decision.

Part of him greatly desired to see Elizabeth again, but their previous encounter unnerved him. So soon into seeing her, his reserve gave way in the worst sort of manner, he found himself unable to control his intentions, and he held her in such an inappropriate manner.

He had held her face in his hands!

He may as well had told the world that they were engaged, with all that he had done. Such an action was as bold as the notion of kissing her.

Ah! To kiss those lips of hers, and to feel their embrace in such a level of blissful intimacy. Such an action would eclipse any thoughts of impediments to their union with each other.

This stream of consciousness made Darcy start.

"Darcy?" Lady Catherine interrupted his thoughts. "You look quite flushed. You are ill. Doctor Grant shall arrive very soon to tend you."

"I thank you, Aunt," Darcy responded, "but it is not necessary. My wrist is merely sprained."

"And to be sure, that is what men always say when they suffer such an accident. And they are never fully well. Doctor Grant shall come, and you will be tended to."

Accepting the wisdom of this, Darcy succumbed to her attentions, and he requested he be excused until then.

Lady Catherine allowed this, and Darcy was offered the serenity of being alone in his guestroom.

Now, his mind could dwell on Elizabeth all that he desired.

No sooner had Darcy been alone that his mind saw a pair of flashing and fine intelligent eyes before him.

He recalled every waking moment of Elizabeth as she had insisted in helping him. So soon his will gave in to her, and Darcy quickly felt regret for his own weakness.

"I should never have come here," he whispered to himself as he sat down in a chair, resting his wrist on the armrest. "What did I expect to occur? Like a moth to a flame."

For truly, what did he expect to happen?

By coming to Rosings, he displayed his own lack of mental clarity. He had not the slightest intention of proposing to Elizabeth.

As far as her fortune, her family, their status, and lacking in connections, she was the worst possible choice for him as a wife.

However, those objections were all from a material point.

On an emotional one, she was perfect for him. Her beauty, which he had dismissed early in their acquaintance, had altered in his views over time. With their acquaintance widening every time that they had met, he grew to know her more. As he discovered more about her, the less he looked on her with indifference and the more he looked on her with pleasure.

And if her beauty was not enough to entice him, which it was, it was cemented by her personality, her behavior, her voice and the way in which she presented herself.

Emotionally, she was his match and perfect for him in every manner.

Alas! The one woman who was ideal for him was also the one woman who was least ideal for him. Life had dealt him quite a blow with that.

So why did he come?

He knew he would never offer her anything, especially since it would be hypocritical. After all, he had advised Mr. Bingley to abandon Jane Bennet for the same reasons that he, Mr. Darcy, would never propose to Elizabeth.

Darcy told himself that it was simple curiosity. He merely needed to see Elizabeth one last time to satisfy himself and be done with this pointless infatuation.

It was the situation in which a moth shall perpetually be drawn towards the very flame that burns it from without and within. And, in some moments, Darcy wondered if Elizabeth was aware of the power she held over him. He began to suspect that she might.

This was his own doing! He ought to have known that his coming was a foolish notion. However, despite the knowledge of knowing things in hindsight, he wondered if he would still have behaved the same way if he could have rewound the past and gone back to being at Canter's Abbey.

Looking down at his hand, he still recalled the time that his hand held her face. Her skin felt warm and soft to the touch, and he fancied himself tied to her in that instant. The more he thought of it, the more he felt as if he could not tell where his skin had begun, and hers ended. But rather, for a brief instant, they had melted into each other, and there was no separation.

Sitting there, Darcy recalled the last time her touch had weakened him, and her power over him eclipsed everything else.

Months ago...

With his valet's assistance, Mr. Darcy was getting dressed in his finest clothes that were best suited for the Netherfield ball. Darcy had never been fully accepting, or content with Bingley's willing eagerness to give a ball in Hertfordshire, for all the plans and preparation that went into it were a burden enough. Even though none of that business was his cross to bear, he still felt the weight pressing upon the occupants at Netherfield for the duration.

Even his fancy clothing still held the sophistication and simplicity that made the Darcy family so respected. His jacket and breeches were black, his tights, waistcoat and cravat were white, and he cut a fine figure when he was finished.

As the guests arrived, Bingley and his sisters stood in line, prepared to meet every person who entered. By just being a guest of the house, Darcy had the luxury of not having to stand there and greet every guest that had arrived.

Therefore, with a philosophical appearance and striking countenance, he was left to the perpetual comfort of standing by a window and looking out of it.

His reasons for remaining there were not from a habit of being disinterested, but rather, he was standing there, in furtive but passionate anticipation for one arrival—the Bennets. Not the entire family, of course, for the parents and youngest daughters were of little to no consequence to him. It was the second eldest, Elizabeth, that he waited for.

Despite his constant attempts to eliminate every secret passion for her, he could not deny that she held some strange power over him. Rather than avoid her at the ball, Darcy had decided that he would not torment himself that night by laboring under the shadow of propriety. Therefore, as soon as the opportunity had presented itself, he would ask her to dance.

Soon, the Bennet carriage arrived, and Elizabeth descended from it. Her family entered Netherfield, and Darcy could see Elizabeth as she removed her coat and was in her ballroom gown.

There, seeing her dressed in a glorious gown that flattered her tremendously, she was the picture of perfection to him.

Darcy stood there, even more frozen than usual, unable to move at the sight of her. In all his life, he wondered if he had ever seen anything so beautiful, so glorious, as she in that moment.

He was in love with her!

The revelation frightened him, and his resolve changed. This realization was so overwhelming, it made him unable to approach her, for he had quite lost his courage.

So, he watched. She entered, and he found that she was frequently being attended to by a man in the company who had a grave appearance about him. His behavior was stiff and reserved, but there was something not very elegant or gallant about his countenance. Darcy hated him on sight. After all the guests had arrived and been met with, Mr. Darcy approached Mrs. Hurst and asked her who the man was. She informed him that he was Reverend William Collins, who was the Bennets' cousin.

As the ball progressed, every now and again, Darcy watched Mr. Collins from out of the corner of his eye, seeing him obviously dote on Elizabeth with marked attention. He hated the man even more than before!

Next, he discovered that Mr. Collins had taken Elizabeth's hand for the first dance.

After this discovery, Darcy secretly wished Mr. Collins to be on the other side of the world and never to have come to Hertfordshire. What was worse was that the man danced so awkwardly. However, this terrible display began to lighten Darcy's mood. For Elizabeth was clearly mortified. The sad state of her dance partner would only augment the pleasure she would have with him when he offered to dance with her.

The more he watched her, the more it became ever apparent

that Elizabeth was doing her very best to enjoy the dance she was having to endure, but that she secretly was indifferent and annoyed with Mr. Collins. Darcy had watched Elizabeth's expressions before enough to know when she was vexed or impatient with something. Or at the very least, he *thought* that he knew her ever so well.

Then the second dance was to come. As Mr. Darcy was preparing himself to walk up to Elizabeth and request her hand for the next set, Mr. Collins had secured her hand for that as well.

Now, Darcy's desires were no longer moderate.

He truly wished that Mr. Collins was dead.

Yes, indeed! This was a very ungenerous and extreme reaction to have. But Darcy was never the sort of man to do things by halves, and his emotions were the same in that regard. Also, when it comes to romance—and all the details and confusion that comes along with it—extreme internal reactions like jealousy and selfishness are naturally the children that are spawned from unsatisfied romance.

Elizabeth was dancing with Mr. Collins.

Therefore, Mr. Darcy was in the most determined state of unsatisfaction. Romantic attachment breeds possessiveness, and he felt possessive over Elizabeth in that moment. And how dare she accept this Mr. Collins to dance with her twice! The foolish man was not worthy of her. Also, she may as well have declared her acceptance of the fact that Mr. Collins desired to marry her. For two dances! That was every indication Mr. Collins was seriously considering Elizabeth in some sort of romantic way.

Darcy could not let this stand. He would dance with her. Come what may!

As soon as her second dance ended with the wretched Collins, Darcy waited until the unwanted reverend was no longer by Elizabeth's side. He saw Elizabeth speaking with Charlotte Lucas, and this offered him no threat. He had met Charlotte Lucas before, had accosted her when she was speaking with Elizabeth, and therefore, he knew he had nothing to lose.

With utter determination, Mr. Darcy marched up to her, and in his usual manner, he looked into her eyes and asked her to dance. Elizabeth's cheeks turned red at the request, and she answered "yes," with alacrity.

This eagerness in agreeing with him was precisely what Darcy wished it would be. She had agreed to dance with him immediately. It was clearly something she was looking forward to immensely.

And he would make certain that she reaped all the joy from it that she could, and that she felt the compliment of being his partner.

The dance had come, and they stood opposite each other as the music began.

She looked beautiful!

The sight of her staring back at him, knowing their hands would touch, and he would have her all to himself for a portion of the hour was enough to overwhelm Darcy.

Now, he was getting nervous.

The dance began. He took her hand, and they began the steps. At the very touch of her, he lost all sense of speech. All he could do was stare back at her as the dance continued.

He stared into her eyes, determined to make his affection felt through the expression that he left unmasked.

I adore you, he felt himself say from within, *Can't you tell?*

After remaining in this state, she was the first to speak.

"We cannot remain in silence throughout this dance," she began, "or I feel that you would despise me greatly by the end."

"Why should I despise you?"

"Silence would make me appear as a taciturn partner, and while silence is something that I know you treasure, I fear that it shall not do for a dance. And I fear the blame of us not speaking together will be laid down at my feet."

"I would never label the lack of conversation as a crime that shall be placed on your name."

"Then, I shall place it upon myself. Let us speak! Or I feel that we may end up being repulsed by the sight of the other one forever."

"I am anxious to speak of what you desire. What would you most like to hear?"

Darcy had very much desired that this response was not only sufficient but desirable. He wanted her to be made aware that he wished to please her. Surely, the sentence could not be mistaken.

"Your reply will do at present," she responded. "For, despite our wishes, no natural conversation can flow from such a beginning. What is natural is now against us. Therefore, we have to choose a subject matter. Should we speak of serious subjects or comical ones?"

"I know that you make it a rule to look for the joke and set it down to base an entire person's character around it."

"You are being ungenerous with me. Then again, you did set me down as being the sort to willfully misunderstand people."

"After you had set it down that I had a propensity to hate everyone around me."

"I speak as I find."

"And with myself, too often, I find as I speak."

"Those sound like the same thing, but are they? That is the question! One seems to be the product of observation and the other the product of happenstance, it happens, and one is lucky that they are correct in how they defined it."

"Do you negate my way of thinking?"

"No, I merely elaborate on it. We are to dance together, and I was enjoying that our conversation had taken a natural turn. For we were not thinking of what we were saying before we said it... we only spoke. Such discourse can be the most comforting kind, even if not the most prudent."

"Perhaps we ought to return to safer subjects. For with subjective perspectives that are off the beaten path of traditional dialogue, I fear that the both of us will find ourselves falling into the side of impropriety."

"And back to prudence, and farewell to surprise. Then let us be silent as we consider what else to talk about."

The dance parted them, and then they returned to each other. Darcy was enjoying himself immensely. But he worried that perhaps he was enjoying himself too much. If they did not remain speaking of general subjects that had no emotional value to them both, then he would be in danger of saying something passionate to her. All had to be guarded.

"Let us talk of travels then," Elizabeth had offered, "and the places we wish to see, or have still not had the pleasure of seeing."

"Where do you wish to roam?"

"Anywhere and everywhere. Seldom has my life taken me further than Meryton. Every now and again, I go to London where my uncle lives, but there is the end of my wanderings."

"I would not know what that sensation is like," he said, "to remain confined to such unvarying society as one neighborhood and a bit of town."

"You are a man, and you have the pleasures of being at liberty to walk, run and roam wherever you wish. Yet we women, as if our lot in life, are to remain safe. A little too safe, in my opinion. We are not at liberty to be driven off to distant lands through our flights of fancy. Therefore, I make a walk to Meryton as eventful as I can."

"And how do you find ways of making such a common, mundane walk to Meryton eventful? For it is a walk that you must make often."

"By putting my entertainment in people, as you know, is often my habit of doing. Especially if there is a new acquaintance to be made, and with the many new people who have entered Hertfordshire, you can tell my fascination is occupied. For, recall the other day, you had met us when we had just been forming a new acquaintance with a gentleman who is to go into the army soon."

Wickham!

The new acquaintance Elizabeth had alluded to came to Darcy's mind very quickly. It had to be Wickham, for he knew Elizabeth could not be referring to anyone else.

"Perhaps you did not remember him," Elizabeth had continued. "For soon after he tipped his hat to you, you had turned your horse and walked down the road."

"I did what was the only option to me at the time," Mr. Darcy had responded.

"The only option? Yes, I heard that you and the gentleman had been previously acquainted. And from what I have gathered, it was a long acquaintance."

"Too long."

"Ah."

"Mr. Wickham is the sort of man who is blessed with happy manners and is sure to always make friends. Whether he is able to keep them is another matter that is quite dubious."

"He had the misfortune to lose your good opinion, and I daresay that it was an unhappy event, and your good opinion of him is lost forever."

"It is, as it ought to be."

"But you are very careful in letting your resentful nature—for resentful you did call your chief flaw—originate? You make sure to bestow your bitter feelings moderately and not too hastily, I take it."

"I do. May I ask to what direction do these questions tend?"

"I am merely trying to illustrate your character, Mr. Darcy, for it is often too hard to make out."

"And what is your success?"

"I do not know," Elizabeth had replied. "For I hear so many different accounts of you as to puzzle me exceedingly."

"I hope to give you more clarity on my nature in the future."

"One cannot know too much about anything. Therefore, I welcome being enlightened."

"Do you really believe that?"

"I do. With all my heart."

They were interrupted by Sir William Lucas.

"I congratulate you, sir," Sir William complimented Mr. Darcy. "Such superior dancing is always a welcome sight, and rarely to be seen. But then, your fair partner is well worthy of you. It would honor us all to see such a display of fine breeding of dance well-repeated—especially when a desirable event is to take place."

When saying this, Sir William looked at Jane and Mr. Bingley, who had been dancing a set together. When seeing Sir William's implications, Mr. Darcy had torn his attention from Elizabeth and looked at his friend. Darcy groaned inwardly. He had been so enraptured with Elizabeth and dancing with her, he did not pay any attention to his friend, or how his friend was displaying his feelings so freely that the world could see it. Darcy had grown lax in his focus.

"What congratulations will then flow in, eh?" Sir William asked.

"Sir," Elizabeth had spoken hesitantly, "I…"

"Nay, no need to explain," Sir William said, pretending as if he would let the secret rest with her. "I understand, I understand. Go on and enjoy the company of each other. Capital! Capital!"

The recollection of Sir William Lucas interrupting their dance with his impertinent remarks about Jane and Bingley had pulled Mr. Darcy from his memories of that ball at Netherfield Park.

That was the first and last time he had the chance to hold Elizabeth's hand to such an extent until this day.

Her touch still lingered on his fingers, the image of her fine eyes rested in the depths of his psyche, and her scent was with him.

Darcy leaned back and rubbed his eyes with his left hand.

"Why is life so very complicated?" he asked himself.

CHAPTER 8

TRIALS & TRIVIALITIES

hen we were returned to Hunsford, we spent time in each other's company, then retired to our rooms where I had the good fortune to sit down and compose a letter.

At this point, Jane was in Cheapside, my uncle and aunt's home, and I wished to appraise her of the news I had encountered Mr. Darcy.

For, now that I had time to reflect on the day's events, I had time to overcome my sensibilities and exercise more sense. Mr. Darcy was Mr. Bingley's bosom friend. Therefore, perhaps there was the chance of me discovering the slightest bit of information about Mr. Bingley, what his state of mind was at the time, and why he had never returned to Netherfield Park. After all, what was there to lose? I was now fatherless, had no prospects on the horizon, and had no desire to marry at present. Also, Mr. Darcy and I had never attempted to desire each other's good opinion before, so what did I have to lose by trying to smooth the way for my sister's path to true love? All in all, Mr. Darcy was the main source through which I could achieve much.

Also, my father had passed away.

After losing him, my slight discord with Mr. Darcy seemed like a trivial matter. It was such a small thing when in comparison with the true tragedies of life.

Ergo, there was a reformation in my mind and a desire to

subdue past offenses. When seeing Mr. Darcy again, I would risk more open communication rather than a guarded discussion. For when was indirection and avoidance of an issue ever the best way that something was achieved? For, looking back on my life, whenever words were not said—when those were words that *ought* to have been said—it was for the benefit of none.

There would be a chance that I was impertinent or too forward in the future. But chances *are* precisely that. Chances! And I would take one now.

Finally, putting pen to paper, I began to write to Jane informing her of all that happened, when suddenly, I heard a knock on my door.

Wrapping my shawl around my nightdress, I asked who it was.

"Tis I," Charlotte responded.

"Come in."

Charlotte, dressed in her robe, entered.

"I had a feeling that you would still be awake," she said, entering and then sitting down on my bed.

"You know me well."

"I had better. Elizabeth, I came for the sake of sounding redundant."

"How so?"

"I want to apologize again. I am sorry for you losing your father."

I lowered my pen down and leaned back in my chair.

"Thank you. I miss him all the time. So, I thank you for inviting me here. By doing so, I can pretend as if he is still alive, and he is home waiting for me. Do you ever feel that way with Mr. Collins?"

Charlotte opened her mouth and then closed it again.

"Never mind," I assured her. "You do not have to answer that question."

"Thank you," she gave way. "For, in a strange way, even when I became a wife, I still saw myself as someone's daughter. And now that I am a widow, I return back to the title I was born into. I can accept this regression of title with ease."

"Why do parents have to die, Charlotte? It is a rhetorical question, I know."

"But we all ask it anyway. It is an unfair thing. Perhaps almost as unfair as when children die. Well, our conversation has taken a turn for the truly serious."

"Even with me, not everything has to be light and breezy."

"It makes you forlorn, of course. And it reminds you that at the end of all things, we will eventually be alone. Death is a very humbling sort of tyrant."

"But it's a tyrant that reminds us we do not have forever. And now that I have become aware that we do not have all the time in the world to do things, I am going to take more initiative in one score."

"And what score is that?"

"I am going to try and make amends with Mr. Darcy."

When hearing this, Charlotte smiled.

"You are going to give him another chance?" Charlotte asked. "You shall attempt to see if he is being agreeable or having changed?"

"Yes, if he chooses to be agreeable or to be changed. However, we do not know that at this time. And you look happy about this?"

"Very much so. That is the reason that I came here to speak with you."

"What?"

"Well, now that Mr. Darcy has returned, I cannot deny that I still believe Mr. Darcy does not despise you, as you think. Perhaps he initially looked on you with a critical eye, but I believe his perspective did not remain there. His view of you seemed to greatly improve over time. Time can prove me wrong, but time can also prove me to be right."

"Well, for the sake of peace and alliance, I would be satisfied with you being correct in this case. Besides, I think I am tired of fighting. I think even my wit is exhausted."

"The loss of your father really is taking its toll on you."

"It has no choice but to. But I will not deny that since time can heal or change many things, that not everything ought to be built on first impressions."

"No, for second impressions, or even third or fourth ones, can have more truth to them. Anyone can start an acquaintance really well, or really poorly. But very few have the skill to maintain an acquaintance and get better with age."

"You think Mr. Darcy is like a fine wine and improves over time?"

"Stranger things have happened. Remember, the Earth was created in six days."

We both chuckled at this acknowledgment.

"Very well," I conceded. "I shall let his actions determine the course of our relationship, for now. Either way, over time, I shall retake the reins and control things, in my own way."

"You would not be Elizabeth if you did anything less."

"But still, I would be Elizabeth if I chose to do more. No, I am slipping somewhere, and I feel it. I missed you being my friend who I could see often."

"I never stopped being that. It was only the distance that separated us."

The next day, we had received an invitation to dine at Rosings Park again, and Sir William and Maria were overjoyed at the news.

I myself was surprised at the sudden desire to have us back at the estate so soon, but we discovered there was a new arrival who was going to be at Rosings. His name was Colonel Richard Fitzwilliam and was Lady Catherine's other nephew whom she had been expecting.

My ever-increasing group of new people to become acquainted with had not reached the point where it was becoming too crowded. Therefore, I was interested in meeting this other nephew, provided his personality was not too similar to Mr. Darcy's. I could withstand Mr. Darcy's habits because time helped me get used to it. But to meet a new man who was like his cousin, I would feel outnumbered.

Therefore, with eagerness, a letter of acceptance was sent, for it was all to be done very quickly. In the afternoon, we visited the great home and found that the new acquaintance had not yet arrived.

"This is most alarming for us," Lady Catherine said to us, "for my dear nephew, the Colonel, should have arrived three hours ago. We worry that something wretched has befallen him, and in an hour, I am sending my fastest man to travel down the road to see if there was any accident on the path that my nephew takes to get here."

"We pray that nothing amiss has occurred," Charlotte spoke for us all, "and I wish that he simply is delayed for innocent and harmless reasons."

"Colonel Fitzwilliam is a strong man," Lady Catherine said, "and I believe that nothing could knock him down. He has survived war. Therefore, I know that nothing on an English road could best him."

"He sounds like a worthy man," I complimented him. "The defenders of Britain can often be the finest set of men in the country."

"Quite so," Sir William found himself able to muster up. "Quite so."

"It depends entirely on the family that they come from," Lady Catherine pointed out. "For if the soldier comes from a poor family, then he is of next to no importance. But my nephew, the Colonel, comes from a great family. Ours is one of the greatest families in all of Britain. Yes, I know the Colonel is well."

"But we still will hope for you, to add to his good fortune," I allowed.

Soon after we sat down, I found myself surprised that Mrs. Jenkinson, who was seated beside Anne de Bourgh, had leaned forward and spoke to me directly.

"Miss Elizabeth," she said, "I heard that you were fond of reading."

Her direct address to me surprised me, but I answered casually.

"It depends on the book," I augmented, "and if its contents like me. If the book loves me, then I make every attempt to love it in return."

"If that be so, then, Lady Catherine, there is a copy of *The Lady of the Lake* that I know would be a particular interest to Miss Bennet. Can I request showing her to the library and pointing the book out to her?"

"Mrs. Jenkinson, there is no need to escort Miss Elizabeth there," Lady Catherine snapped. I got the feeling that she did not like the idea of me being led around the house instead of remaining there where she could oversee everything I said and did. "Just get the book yourself and bring it to her."

"Yet, Lady Catherine, there are a few copies of the book, and perhaps Miss Elizabeth would like to choose from among the editions."

It was strange, but I got the sense that Mrs. Jenkinson had some other motive for wanting me to see the library. Despite my being ignorant of why, I followed my intuition and decided to trust her.

"Yes," I augmented, and I saw Lady Catherine's eyes grow wide. I had to think quickly. Then it occurred to me, what affected Lady Catherine most was pride and her vanity. To influence her, I had to swell her vanity and inflate it to large proportions. "Also, Lady Catherine, I have heard that your library is one of the best in England."

"That is an understatement. It is the *best* in Britain."

For a brief second, I flinched under such conviction of her boast, but I soon recovered.

"Then, under the steady and sound eyes of Mrs. Jenkinson, I would love to see this library and be allowed the fortune of viewing this legendary copy of the book in a peaceful manner. Please, I desire to see your library, and I am interested in the book."

"Your request is so pressing for so young a person and for a stranger in a home, but I shall and can easily see the source of it. You are overjoyed at being in Rosings, and it has overwhelmed your sense. Mrs. Jenkinson, you may escort Miss Bennet to our library, show her the book, and when it is decided which copy that she wishes to choose to borrow, return here instantly."

Mrs. Jenkinson nodded.

"I thank you, Lady Catherine, for your kindness."

Together, Mrs. Jenkinson and I left the sitting room where the others were.

CHAPTER 9

TWO PEOPLE OF A TACITURN NATURE

*T*ogether, we walked along, and I felt Mrs. Jenkinson and I made a strange pair. We had barely spoken two words to each other before she recommended the book to me.

"This copy that Rosings has must be a special find."

"I suppose it may be," she responded. This response immediately exposed that it was not the book that we were walking towards.

"Yes," I said. "I suppose it may."

We reached the library and entered it.

"I assume that you would be so kind as to stay with me while I choose the book," I said, "and where in the shelves is it located?"

"It shall be on the table by the window against the wall," Mrs. Jenkinson said, pulling a copy of *Grimm's Fairy Tales* from the shelf. "I shall be on the other side of the room while you are making your choice."

With that, she left me alone, chose a chair and desk as far from me as she could, and sat down with her back towards me.

Curious behavior.

From the other side of the room, I heard the scratching away of something. Moving towards it, I was letting my curiosity get the best of me. Soon, I deduced that it sounded like a quill scratching away on a paper.

Reaching the end of a set of shelves, I turned the corner and saw

Mr. Darcy sitting at a desk. His right hand was wrapped in bandages with a splint attached to it to keep him from bending it. As I looked on him, I saw him writing—with his left hand.

"You are left-handed?" I asked.

Hearing me, he stopped writing and turned around.

"Ah, Mrs. Jenkinson was able to retrieve you," he said, but then he recalled what I had observed. "And no, I am not left-handed."

"But you are writing with your left hand."

"I am merely scribbling down some notes that I have to send to my housekeeper back at Pemberly. I felt I ought to write them down so I did not forget them."

Looking over his shoulder, I saw the letters were relatively even, despite that they were smeared every now and again. But that was easy to account for. If you wrote with your left hand, then you were guaranteed to smear the letters sometimes by your palm touching the paper.

"A person could not write letters that even unless they were left-handed originally," I noted, taking a step forward. "Were you born left-handed?"

Mr. Darcy leaned back in his seat; his eyes fixed on me.

"Yes," he confessed, "I was. But as a child, I was properly reprimanded for it, so now I write with my right hand. I am only using my left hand now because I have to keep my other wrist still."

"Because of me."

"I do not mean to have you feel guilt. Having time to reflect, we both can call it a mere accident."

"For it was one," I teased, "thank you, sir, for you are generous in your decision-making."

His eyes twinkled at this.

"Anyway," I continued, "I never judge left-handed people. It was never their fault that they were born that way. In the end, we just have to be who we are. Of course, I am happy that you learned to write with your right hand, for it makes letter-writing neater and less-smeared. Forgive me for being impertinent, but I have been curious. What is it like to be born left-handed?"

Mr. Darcy looked down at the floor.

"That was a foolish question," I admitted, "and I need no answer."

"No, it is not a foolish question. It is simply that no one has ever asked me that before. Not even my parents."

"Did your sister know you were?"

"No. By the time she was born, I had already learned to write with my right hand. Well, being born left-handed...it is to be born with what can only be regarded as a defect. A slight one, but still a defect, nonetheless. It is to be born wrong."

"Did you feel wrong?"

"Yes, I did. My parents were very gentle in what they said to me about it, but I do recall feeling a sort of shame about it when I was young."

"Never fear. I am certain they were proud of you. Though, my condolences for having gone through that. If it helps, being born left-handed perhaps is the same sort of situation of being born not-so-handsome when you are a woman. Beauty is something that one wishes to obtain if they possibly can. And when we do not, that is the worst sort of defect, for it is a permanent one."

"When have you ever known such a defect?"

"My entire life."

"I cannot believe that."

"Very much, you can. For you have seen my elder sister. Living one's life under such a paragon is never so easy. And you lived under the weight of left-handed people. It explains something about your nature."

"Does it?"

"At a young age, you were corrected. Corrections leave scars."

He and I both looked at each other, and then I realized we had never arrived at the point and purpose for our meeting.

"So," I began, "I take it that you were the cause for Mrs. Jenkinson requesting the book. And are you still there, Mrs. Jenkinson?" I called over my shoulder.

"I always do my duty to the best of my ability," Mrs. Jenkinson called from her seat. "That means I never leave a young lady unchaperoned when she's not in mixed company."

"And you do your service well," Mr. Darcy responded, then he lowered his breath and whispered to me. "I pay her five pounds for her services."

"I never knew you were the furtive and clandestine sort," I whispered in response, "but I suppose money can buy many things."

Mr. Darcy did not say anything again, and we were on the verge of once more sinking into silence.

"May I sit down?" I asked.

"Yes," he rushed out, remembering himself, "pray, do be seated."

"That is very good," I said, sitting down a short distance from him. "Because we do not have very much time, and I can assume that you sent for me for a reason."

"Yes. I worry that I did not give the best first impression after the accident, and I wanted you to know that I thank you for your assistance."

"You are welcome, but it was the least I could do. For I was the reason that you fell off your horse, to begin with. And is your hand in much pain?"

"A cold compress was made for it; therefore, I feel less pain. However, it is still best that I do not move it."

"I would offer you my services to help you if you ever needed use of a right-handed person, but I believe that important men such as yourself have a valet about who spends their life doing as you bid."

"Do you toy with me when you mention my valet?"

"I can make a toy of any subject matter. With you, I cannot deny that I have never met a man who others are often so easily at his disposal. You can move people about with dangerous influence."

"Dangerous?"

"Whenever a man or woman has much power over so many people, it can be either harmonious or dangerous. You have to understand that I have a right to proceed with caution when I meet men like you. For I do not know on which side of the situation do you fall. Are you harmonious or dangerous?"

"Do I look dangerous?"

"Not everything that is dangerous looks it. You look like a

gentleman, but clothes can always remedy a villain underneath. Give me time, Mr. Darcy, and let me decide on my own."

Once more, he did not say anything in return.

"Well," I concluded, "if we are finished speaking, then would you point me in the direction of *The Lady of the Lake*? With your aunt, nothing is below her scrutiny."

"There is one other thing."

"Yes?"

"Is it true?"

"Is what true?"

"Is your father gone?"

I swallowed and looked down.

"While my father is never far from my thoughts," I admitted, somber, "yes, he is gone."

"I know the pain of losing one's parent," he said.

"Yes, you lost your father a few years ago, did you not?"

"Indeed, I did. We never are fully whole after it, are we?"

"No, we are not. It also reminds us that we have no choice but to not have everything. Does it ever feel unfair to you that life has to be such a way?"

"Yes, I feel the unevenness of eternity quite often."

"I know, compared to some, we have no right to complain."

"No, there is no reason to do that. There is no reason for being silent on such grief just because others have more misfortunes. We have the right to speak of when a loved one is lost to us."

"I miss him, Mr. Darcy. As you perhaps miss your father and mother."

"Yes. We are now kindred in spirit. At least…we are not alone in that way."

"I suppose you to be right. I almost did not come to Hunsford because of it, but I was pressed. I suppose that it served me correct, for I said the same news to my sister."

"Which sister?"

"Jane. She has gone to London to stay with our aunt and uncle for a time. Have you never happened to see her when she was there?"

Mr. Darcy's eyes shifted, he looked down at the ground, and then he looked back at me.

"No, I have not had the pleasure."

"Oh," I responded. There was something in his manner for which I did not trust entirely. "Well, do you give me leave to extend your condolences to her as well? It will fill her heart to hear your kind words."

"Of course, you may."

"Thank you. Due to your sudden departure from Netherfield Park, she never got the chance to give you all a proper farewell. Your company was missed."

"By her, or by you as well?"

"I make it a habit to only miss the company of those who I know shall miss my company as well. There is no point in feeling something if there is no hope of the emotion being reciprocated."

"I do not believe in that philosophy. Sometimes, a person cannot help but feel an emotion, even if they are not certain the other person feels in the same manner. After all, not everything starts out as a reaction to something. Some things start out as an action that springs up from its own origins."

"Your point works for others, but it will not do for my own practices. I refuse to bestow my feelings on someone who I am certain may not care for them. When you all left, did you ever write to us? Did your company ever extend any invitations for us to visit you all when you were in town?"

"Well," he bit his lip, "it may not have been a prudent step to do so."

"What is right to do can never be done too quickly. Those in Mr. Bingley's company, who had felt an intimacy with her, should have written. She missed them. And she felt deeply for them."

Turning around, I went to the library shelves and found the copy of 'Lady of the Lake' on my own.

"Never mind, I found the book myself."

"Are you desirous to get away from me?" he asked suddenly.

"No, I am just desirous of not hearing your aunt chastise me for taking so long."

"You are afraid of my aunt?"

"No, never! I merely am afraid of her saying something to me that will provoke me to say something harsh in return. That would be a scene that should never arise at Rosings Park."

Walking up to Mrs. Jenkinson, I bowed my head.

"Thank you for recommending this poem," I added, "I shall enjoy it."

"You are most welcome," she responded, standing up and leading me back to the sitting room. "For nothing is ever more innocent than recommending a book to someone."

CHAPTER 10

MY SECRET SOUL

$\mathcal{A}$s we walked back to the sitting room, I looked out of a window, and I saw a rider approaching Rosings. He was wearing the traditional habit of a gentleman, and when he got closer, I pointed.

"Mrs. Jenkinson, would that be Colonel Fitzwilliam?"

"Yes," Mrs. Jenkinson replied, "it is! Oh, Lady Catherine would be ever so happy to see him."

"And to learn that he hasn't been kidnapped by gypsies either," I smirked. "But he is alive and whole."

As we stood there, Colonel Fitzwilliam reached the front of the house. A servant took his horse away, and he dismounted, taking the front steps two at a time.

"He always was of a lively nature," Mrs. Jenkinson commented.

"You seem to think well of him," I observed.

"You will, as well."

We continued to walk along the hallway that was at the top of the steps, just as Colonel Fitzwilliam entered and was greeted by the butler at the front door. When stepping in, Colonel Fitzwilliam was immediately removed of his hat and coat while also taking off his gloves. After smiling at the butler, he clearly sensed something about him. Turning, he faced Mrs. Jenkinson and me from the top of the steps.

Despite that we had not been introduced, he smiled at me.

"I see that we have mice in the house," he laughed.

"Colonel," Mrs. Jenkinson gasped, "you cannot speak to a lady who you have not been introduced to yet, you rogue. Just as you cannot be calling ladies mice."

"Thank you for restoring order and decorum for us, Mrs. Jenkinson," I smiled, "but I do not mind. Is this Colonel Fitzwilliam that we see now?"

"Yes, it is indeed," Mrs. Jenkinson grinned.

"Yes, it is indeed," Colonel Fitzwilliam echoed as if he were a parrot.

"Then can you introduce us?" I asked Mrs. Jenkinson. "For if you do not do so quickly, then we shall be forever breaking the rules."

"I shall spare you both and bring you away from the edges of impropriety," Mrs. Jenkinson said. "Colonel, this is Miss Elizabeth Bennet, who is a guest at Hunsford Parsonage. Miss Bennet, this is Colonel Richard Fitzwilliam, Lady Catherine's other nephew."

"Who offended everyone with his lateness," Colonel Fitzwilliam admitted.

"But I believe he will be forgiven quickly," I offered.

"You shall bring levity to the party," Mrs. Jenkinson complimented him. "For your aunt is in one room, lamenting your absence, and your cousin Darcy is in the library, in isolation as he is recovering from an injury that was procured from his falling off his horse."

"Good god, is Darcy alright?" Colonel Fitzwilliam asked, his tone changing to concern and gentle alarm.

"He is well. His wrist is merely sprained and needs isolation to recover."

"Then I am torn, for I do not know which relative to go to first. Either way, I offend one."

"Which one is your instinct to visit first?" I asked.

Colonel Fitzwilliam's eyes twinkled when he looked on me.

"That is an unfair question. For if I do answer in favor of one, then I bestow the compliment on them by slighting the other."

"And that was the perfect answer," I assured him. "Any other response would have cast you in a bad light."

"Is the sun still shining on me?"

"Does it still shine on the British Empire?" I asked, refusing to answer his question.

He chuckled, then he turned to Mrs. Jenkinson.

"Mrs. Jenkinson," he cooed, "I need your light touch. Deliver me unto my aunt and help me make my apologies for making her afraid on my account."

Mrs. Jenkinson led him forward. I remained to one side of her while Colonel Fitzwilliam remained on her other side. They both spoke with animation and familiarity. It was clear that he was a favorite of hers.

And Colonel Fitzwilliam being a favorite did not end with Mrs. Jenkinson, but only began there.

When he entered the room, Lady Catherine chided him on his tardiness. He explained himself with ease and grace in his tone. His horse had merely had a defective horseshoe. The Colonel had to break his journey at a smithy shop to have it repaired, and then he set out again immediately.

While he finished his explanation, offered his apologies to us and made our acquaintance, his character was quick to disassemble. He was not as handsome as Mr. Darcy, and not half as handsome as Mr. Wickham, but for some reason, it did not matter at all.

He was blessed, by nature, with an ease of manner that gave him a comfortable air. There are those that we meet in our lives who, for some reason, are more comfortable to be around than others, and we never can explain the power they have over us. Colonel Fitzwilliam quickly was that sort of person. When he walked into the room, he was able to bring a comfort that could only be felt rather than explained. There seemed to be a pleasantness about his mouth as he spoke, and Charlotte, Maria and Sir William were as happy to be near him as Lady Catherine was.

In fact, we perhaps were more so because after Lady Catherine asked him every question that could be asked of him, he turned to us and presented a variety of subjects that put us at ease.

First, he inquired about Sir William and wondered if his knighthood had been presented at St. James's Court.

With a subject so familiar to him, Sir William was able to gather his courage and talk animatedly of the day that he was knighted. Now and again, Lady Catherine gave her input on this and that, but even she allowed Sir William to speak much without being interrupted.

Next, Colonel Fitzwilliam turned his attention to Maria and I, asking us about Hertfordshire, how did we like Hunsford, and if we were as comfortable there as we were in our home county.

Maria answered back in the affirmative, stating that she was even more in wonder at Rosings than she ever would be at home.

I admitted I could not be so partial.

"Kent has Rosings Park," I said, "and lovely woods and hills, which should automatically give it all the advantages. However, despite that Hertfordshire and Meryton are not as lovely, home shall always be home. Your home, Chatsworth, naturally can objectively have the advantages of being foremost in your mind as superior to anywhere else, because it is your home and also naturally elegant. Although, with Longbourn, I know that it is not so great a house. But it is still my home. And therefore, I like it better than anywhere else."

"This perspective of yours has the habit of being blinded by preference for one's own home," Lady Catherine said. "That is very natural and perhaps very proper. But the longer you remain in Kent, you shall find very few places inferior to it or even on its level. You shall be sad when going away from Rosings and, I daresay, not even want to return home."

"Time shall tell," was all that I replied with.

"Now," Colonel Fitzwilliam announced, standing up, "propriety commands that I visit my injured cousin, who I was informed is in another part of the house, recovering gracefully."

"Very well," Lady Catherine permitted, "but if Darcy is on the mend, tell him he can join us when you are to return."

"I shall deliver the message with eagerness," he grinned, and then he left the room.

His absence was immediately felt. Truly, it felt as if a small source of electric energy had evaded us. Lady Catherine continued to speak, but I wondered if our presence antagonized her. Naturally, we could not have been as important to her as the Colonel or Darcy, but she continued to speak on until it was time for our departure.

I wished to have seen the Colonel again before we left, but it was not to be so.

However, my chief consolation was that Mr. Darcy and I had met each other again, and our conversation was sanguine. There was no hostility in our tone, and perhaps, in the end, we could at least meet each other as common acquaintances.

The next day, no invitation from Rosings Park came, and I knew the reason. With her nephews at Rosings, Lady Catherine would have entertainment that was dearer to her heart.

And perhaps it was better, for it would have looked indelicate of her to invite us when her other nephew may still have been infirm.

The next day brought letters, and letters are always a welcome thing.

Two of those letters were equally as interesting, but one had a more favorable bit of information than the other.

The first was from Longbourn, and the letter was sent from Kitty herself.

Dear Lizzy,

Mama and the rest of us have received your last letter with satisfaction. While I never despised Charlotte Lucas or even Mr. Collins for their actions in marrying each other, I did always comprehend our mother's frequent uncharitable views on them.

When we read your letter and the news of Charlotte's childless state became known, mama was elated, and she expressed the first kind words that she has had about Charlotte in the last year. Now that we are currently out of danger, her nerves are less trying for her. And now, I no longer have to despair of her reprimanding me for when I begin to have a cough. Truly, how does my coughing vex her

*when it is not something that I can help? Lizzy, I cannot help but feel
as if everyone can be a little unkind to me.*

Kitty's letter broke off at a certain point, and it was clear that
she had started writing it, then something took her away from the
activity, and now she was returning to it.

*Lizzy, something has happened since I last began to write that will
shock you. However, the shock will give way, and you will be very
relieved. I wish I was there at present to see your face, for I believe
that you shall blush.*

Mr. Wickham is not to marry Mary King, after all.

*Risking his reputation as being inconstant, it has been made
public that he has withdrawn his offer of marriage from Mary King.
Her uncle, who had come down from Liverpool, has called him out
on Wickham's ill-behavior to his poor niece. Wickham apologized for
the mistreatment that he has cast Mary King in, however, he
remained firm. He also offered, to Mary King's uncle, to meet the next
day, for a duel. They would fight, and Wickham would let her uncle
fight for his niece's honor.*

*I, nor any lady that I know of, were present at the time, but
many soldiers were, and there were even a few servants who spied the
event from the woods along Sheraton hill.*

*The way the story goes is that Mr. Wickham did present himself,
on time, for the duel. Mary King's uncle also appeared, and swords
were presented. But rather than fight, Mr. Wickham threw down his
sword, knelt down in front of Mary's uncle, and unbuttoned his coat.*

*He offered permission for Mary's uncle to take his revenge, bearing
his soul for her uncle to do with what he wished. However, Mr. King
hesitated. Wickham was witnessed stating afterward that his
principal reason for revoking his offer of marriage was because he
realized that he was not worthy of Mary King. She had a fortune,
and he was virtually penniless. Having let his flights of fancy get
ahead of his senses, he had been careless in making her an offer when
he brought so little to the marriage.*

*For, his actions, despite any honorable intentions that he may
have had, would appear as the worst sort of mercenary intentions and*

would present him as too much of a fortune hunter. Mary King, by his declaration, deserved better than what he was originally going to propose. Mr. King, seeing the wisdom and good nature behind this action, realized that Mr. Wickham's actions were done out of a desire for self-sacrifice.

Therefore, the duel ended with no sword's point being thrust into a man's chest but ended in kind words offered on both sides. Mr. King left with his niece's integrity intact, and Mr. Wickham left, even more loved than before.

Is this all not a fantastic thing?

I find it to be so.

Truly, I wish for you to be here, so that I may chuckle at how you receive this news. Now, Mr. Wickham is single, unmarried, and there for you to fall in love with again.

Your heart still has one option open, but Lydia has now also begun to hope. I know that you would think that I am heartbroken about this, however, in truth, I am not. I enjoyed Mr. Wickham, but I secretly make it a rule to not fancy men that my other sisters like. It hardly seems like something that would make sense when it comes to sisterly affection. Therefore, I may make declarations about Mr. Wickham's beauty, but I only admire and do not feel.

Therefore, this news shall be left to you and Lydia of who values it more.

But Mr. Wickham is single again, under the most incredible of circumstances. I have read novels that did not contain events such as these. It does give me hope for the future that, one day, life is often allowed to be so very imaginative!

Yours, etc.

Kitty

When I closed the letter back up again, I instinctively hid it away in my luggage.

Could this all be true?

Mr. Wickham really did break off his engagement to Miss King? And then, as a gentleman, he offered himself up to Mr. King's mercy, willing to allow himself to be chastised for the sake of honor.

Mr. King's behavior was everything that was appropriate and worthy of an uncle who was protecting his niece's honor, so both men were now above reproach.

Though Mr. Wickham's actions toward Miss King were not always so terribly innocent, I could not think of that right now, in light of the heroic manner in which he acted afterward.

For a brief moment, I felt sorry for Miss King. For a man retracting his offer of marriage can sometimes be regarded as humiliating. And the woman would be called out to spoil because she would be labeled as a woman who could not convince a man to continue feeling affection for her. However, with Mr. Wickham's blatant confession that he was not worthy of her fortune, perhaps that knowledge would soften the blow she was dealt and keep people from cruelly ridiculing her.

For my part, I could not think on her too greatly, for Mr. Wickham showed something even greater than perfection now. He displayed the actions of a man who committed to a decision, realized that perhaps his actions were too mercenary and were not respectful to the feelings of the woman he was about to use to his advantage. Rather than casually continue on this road—which would be the easiest thing in the world to do—he confronted his actions himself and removed himself from the situation before he could do any more damage.

Not all of us had it in us to be perfect.

Yet all of us had the ability to confront the imperfection which was within us and try to overcome it. It was simply that most of us did not ever take the pains of improving our own nature. Mr. Wickham had done the feats that were the emotional equivalent to that of Heracles.

Therefore, my respect for him had now increased, which startled me, because how could they have gotten higher than what they were already? But now, all men paled in comparison to him even more, and all their manhoods could be regarded as cheap for not being on his level.

But to break off an engagement that was so advantageous on his side. What could have inspired such a strong moral decision?

A part of me wished to attribute it to his deep and moral abilities. He truly was a wonderful marvel of a man.

Or was there more to his reasoning? Perhaps he broke off the engagement because he had developed a passionate attachment to another woman?

Forgive my vanity, but could that woman have been me? Soon after having the idea, I dismissed the notion immediately. Then, as a moth to a flame, it kept returning to the forefront of my mind. Could this all have occurred because Mr. Wickham's attachment to me was stronger than I had reasoned?

If so, then this was all my fault!

Mr. Wickham was the sort of man who I found charming, agreeable, handsome and very striking. I was drawn to him. But was it love I was ever feeling? I felt flattered by his attentions, and perhaps, in being so, I displayed my affection for him a little too clearly. However, I could not have helped it. He was captivating.

I was not so certain that I ever could fully feel a truly deep attraction to him that would render me in love. After all, when I had heard he was to be married, I did not feel any protestations originating from any sort of jealousy. If I had been in love, wouldn't I have been irate over his actions? Would I not have felt a deep and painful resentment to Miss King and towards Mr. Wickham?

But I had not. I wished him well and only felt like I was losing his company. And my chief reason for expressing any sort of sentiment when he said that if he were wealthy, he might have chosen me, was because I was flattered by his attentions. Yet, here and now, with him being single, I was worried. If his designs toward me were now serious, then I would not know how to respond.

Maybe I was in love with him, but since I was not used to the emotion, then maybe I did not know that I had fully begun to have it.

I would let his actions be my guide. If he broke off his engagement solely because he realized that there was no real affection in the case, and he could not make Miss King happy, then I would be overjoyed. Yet, if his sole reason for remaining single were because of me, then I would remain on my guard.

Maybe, over time, I could love him. It would be an imprudent match on both sides. Neither he nor I would be entering the arrangement with a fortune. We both could offer each other nothing.

Despite all this, I was certain I could learn to economize when it came to our living conditions. Also, perhaps, now that Longbourn might still be ours, we could safely remain there, and Mr. Wickham could gain some useful employment.

Maybe, in some manner, he could even be given Longbourn? After all, there was no male heir now to come forward and claim it. Therefore, if it were to fall into the hands of our Uncle Gardiner or Uncle Phillips, then I was certain they would have no scruples on giving it to my husband.

Who knew?

Perhaps time would tell. All of my worries and confusion could have easily been for nothing. He might never make me an offer, and my consideration of him doing so would be merely attributed to my own vanity.

Dismissing the first letter from my mind, I picked up the next letter and saw that it was from Jane.

Eager to discover what news there was from Gracechurch Street —and happy to separate my mind from Mr. Wickham's predicament—I picked up the letter and began to read its contents:

My dearest Lizzy,

You, I am sure, will be incapable of triumphing on your better judgment, at my expense, when I confess myself to have been entirely deceived in Miss Bingley's regard for me. But, my dear sister, though the event has proved you right, do not think me obstinate if I still assert that, considering what her behavior was, my confidence was as natural as your suspicion. I do not at all comprehend her reason for wishing to be intimate with me, but if circumstances were to happen again, I am sure I should be deceived again.

As you know, a few weeks ago, I called on Miss Bingley and Mrs. Hurst at their home, visiting them to pay my respects. I was glad to see Caroline again, and I thought she was a little glad to see me, but a little out of spirits. She chastised me for not writing to her, and I informed her that I had sent two letters to her. She made it clear she had never received the letters at all. I found it ever so odd that both of my letters should go astray, but stranger things have happened.

After calling on her, she and Mrs. Hurst assured me they would return my visit with one of their own. Therefore, I waited every morning at home for two weeks to see them.

Then, at length, Miss Bingley came, but she did not return my visit till yesterday, and not a note, not a line, did I receive in the meantime. When she did come, it was very evident she had no pleasure in seeing me. She made a slight, formal apology for not calling before, said not a word of wishing to see me again, and was in every respect so altered a creature that when she went away, I was perfectly resolved to continue the acquaintance no longer. Forgive me, but I cannot help blaming her. If she were only to forget me soon after we parted ways, then she was very wrong for singling me out the way she did. I can safely say that every advance to intimacy began on her side.

Perhaps she does it because she has anxiety over the situation of me and her brother? For, she knows that any affection he had for me has now quite gone away.

For, when I asked about her brother, she made it evident to me he very well knows of my being in town but has long been enjoying the company of Miss Darcy as well as other friends of his. I can conclude then that Mr. Bingley now no longer cares for me.

Naturally, that would make Caroline apprehensive around me. For perhaps, she was aware of my warm regard for him, and knowing that my feelings are not returned, she does not know how to look on me.

Oh, Lizzy, can there be any other way to determine her coldness now? Either way, I do believe, sister, you were correct about her all this time. My shame of being duped is complete, but I take comfort in that I did all in my power to be above reproach.

For, the only crime that I can attribute to myself is embarrassment. Is that ever so terrible?

Yet, other than this news, London is diverting, and I am happy to be here with my generous and kind aunt and uncle. With the exception of missing you terribly, and our good family, I can attest that I am recovering now.

Father's death still affects me, but I can bear it now, for our aunt and uncle fill up the vacancy that he has left behind. In truth, I love living with them, and I want for nothing now.

I am well and we all make a merry company here.

Yours etc.
Jane

As I folded up the letter, many emotions came to me.

I was sorry for Jane's situation, for I had hoped that her going to town would help her learn anything of Mr. Bingley's plight, and they could reunite.

But of Miss Bingley's behavior, I was left completely unsurprised. I always knew that Caroline Bingley's regard was a flimsy one at best and a selfish one at worst. My sister was beautiful and had a lovely nature. Therefore, being a person in Hertfordshire worth knowing, Jane was perfect for Miss Bingley's and Mrs. Hurst's taste. Everything about Jane recommended her to them, but it was a vain sort of friendship. Their attachment to Jane was purely circumstantial. They were in the country; therefore, they were idle and needed someone who could fill up their time and curiosity. But now that they were in town, and there were more important people to meet, my sister fell to the wayside of their interest and was not worth their kind. In *their* eyes, this concept of friendship was logical. I had met their kind before.

However, Jane had made a valid point. Perhaps Miss Bingley's attitude had altered so drastically toward Jane *because of Mr. Bingley*. After all, if their brother no longer cared for Jane, then the Bingley sisters naturally would feel discomfort around Jane, for they knew their brother had abandoned all affection for her.

However, I dismissed this notion as soon as I had thought it. After all, even Jane now was aware of their true nature. If Miss Bingley really had felt true amicability toward her, then would Miss Bingley have cared very much that her brother did not love Jane? If she were governor of her own feelings and ruler of her own thoughts, then Miss Bingley would not have let her brother's lack of a romantic regard for Jane lessen her in her eyes. If anything, she would have pitied Jane for Mr. Bingley's choosing to forget about her. Yet, she clearly did not. Therefore, her affection for Jane was either never real, or it never rested in its proper place.

However, I was still not going to believe that Mr. Bingley was not in love with Jane. His expressions were too marked, his attentions to her too real… in the same way that it could be supposed that Mr. Wickham once looked on me.

In the same way that Mr. Wickham once looked on me.

The comparison was not lost on me that both men did look on Jane and I fondly, and ultimately offered us nothing afterward. Yet, Mr. Wickham had now relinquished Mary King, and Mr. Bingley's true relationship to Miss Darcy was still not known. Therefore, there was still hope for Jane and Mr. Bingley.

Time was showing me that nothing was over until it was fully over.

Jane's time was not yet done.

And once more, I was sure that there was some trickery, mischief and deceit involved.

Miss Bingley was hiding something. She had some part to play in all this, and Mrs. Hurst perhaps did as well. Jane may have been amusing to them as a passing friend, but she was not the ideal candidate for their brother, and therefore, they were desirous to separate Jane and Bingley.

Of this, I was sure.

However, as I sat the letter down, my mind wandered over to Mr. Darcy.

I recalled the day before when I had mentioned my sister, and he looked away from me before answering.

He knew more than he was letting on.

I knew that he knew more than he was letting on.

And, in the most tactless way that I could achieve my own ends, I would discover the truth.

For life was short. Therefore, what did I have to lose?

CHAPTER 11

AMICABILITY

*T*he next day, as I was composing my letters to Jane and Kitty, we had received two visitors.

Colonel Fitzwilliam visited, and with him came Mr. Darcy.

Both men bowed, exchanged pleasantries, and the conversation commenced well enough.

"We also come with an errand," Colonel Fitzwilliam informed us as he took his seat closest to me, his eyes twinkling. "Our Aunt, the *right and honorable* Lady Catherine, would be very honored if you were to dine with us this evening."

"Oh," Maria cried, turning to her father and Charlotte, "may we please go?"

"Of course, we should," Sir William confirmed, "for we have no fixed engagements."

"Indeed, we do not," Charlotte added, "therefore, yes, we would love to dine at Rosings this evening."

"Good," Colonel Fitzwilliam responded, crossing his legs, "though, if we were all to be honest with each other, I do not believe that all of you really had any choice in the matter. If you did not agree, our aunt may have sent hounds after you all."

We all laughed.

"That is the way of family," I added, "not speaking directly of your aunt, but some family members speak poniards, and every word stabs."

"How Shakespearean of you to say that."

"There is a little bit of Shakespeare in all of us, I gather."

"I can well believe it. What do you say, Darcy?"

"I say that it all matters what character from Shakespeare is it that we are most like," Mr. Darcy responded, standing by the window. "Tragic, historic or comedic?"

"I do not believe that you or I could be one or the other," I pointed out. "Or anyone for that matter. Rather, I find us to be an amalgamation of many characters. Each day, it's always a surprise of which one we shall wake up as."

"That gives us comfort then," Colonel Fitzwilliam responded, "for if all of us have a tragic character in us, it shows an inevitability of being malicious sometimes, and showing that we have no choice."

"Are you confessing to having a dark side to your nature? I never would have suspected it in a man such as you."

"Truly," Charlotte supported me, "the confessions of a Colonel are surprising us today."

"Men such as yourself command such gentlemanly manners," Sir William compiled, "that the concept of you having anything in common with *Macbeth* must render us shocked."

"*Macbeth* and *Othello*, perhaps not," Colonel Fitzwilliam said, "but with *Hamlet*, now, I admit that perhaps there is a side to me that is a pale shadow of that mood. Despite our natures to always be civil, each of us has a darkness in us that, when revealed, is quite alarming."

After he said this, I stole a quick glance at Mr. Darcy, who seemed to appear as nervous and was scratching his neck. He stole a glance at me as well, and then looked down at the floor.

"My, my, my," Maria sighed, nervous, "this conversation has taken a turn that has overwhelmed me. For I know not what to say."

We all laughed at this.

"And speaking of tragedy," I added, "what of you, Mr. Darcy? We see you have recovered."

"Yes, and I believe the recovery is complete," he responded. "I woke up today with no pain."

"We are glad to hear of it," Charlotte responded, "however, you have done nothing to exert yourself too far, I hope. If you use your arm again so soon after recovery, there can always be a relapse."

"Thank you for your concern."

"I warned him in the same style," Colonel Fitzwilliam compiled, "therefore, it is agreed between us. Whenever he needs something lifted that is heavier than a feather, I can supply the labor."

"Spoken like a military man," I pointed out. "Between your cousin and yourself, you both paint a contrast of two different specimens of Englishmen."

"Have you ever been wounded in battle, Colonel?" Maria asked.

"Maria, that is an impertinent question," Charlotte whispered.

"I am starved by my curiosity, that is all," Maria rushed out, "I apologize."

"Oh, but it is fine," the Colonel responded, "I am, in truth, flattered that you even inquired about it. Too often, people shy away from the graver and more frightening aspects of the darker sides of life." Here, he turned to Charlotte and Sir William. "Sometimes, what must be talked about is not proper for society, but it still must be talked about all the same. Yes, I have been wounded in battle before. I was once shot in my left arm and received a stab wound in my leg."

Maria and Charlotte covered their mouths, but I leaned forward, curious.

"That happened?" I asked, "And yet, here you are."

"Yes, here I am."

"The gunshot and the stabbing...the pain was excruciating, and that must have felt like true horror to you."

"Oh, yes. They were the two most painful things that I have ever endured."

"And yet you have the ability and strength to continue to remain in the army," Charlotte added, "despite knowing the horrors that await you."

"It must be from a firm love for your country," Sir William declared, "and England is proud to have men such as yourself."

"I thank you for your compliment," Colonel Fitzwilliam said, "yet, in truth, I do not deserve it."

"How could you do yourself an injustice?" I asked.

"Because it is true. The reason that I fight is not because of my patriotic pride, although such pride does exist within me. No, in truth, it is simply that I have no other talent and no other notion of what to do in life. Therefore, I do this, for it is simply the only way that I can achieve my living."

Naturally, his confession made us all admire him, but it also created an awkwardness.

I was certain that we all felt a sense of shame now, in comparison with the Colonel's life. We all complained or wondered how our lives could be improved. But between the Colonel's history and my father's death, I wondered how much we humans truly allowed ourselves to live?

"The price of being born as we are," I acknowledged to the Colonel. "Is it not a frightening thing? The cost of being alive is to possibly endanger ourselves to do it."

"Yes, it does seem a little cruel," Colonel Fitzwilliam responded, "but I refuse to let our company lose its life and gaiety because of me." His eyes twinkled. "I live, I breathe, and I thrive, so let us fill our conversations with the charming trivialities that make life so busy."

We all laughed at this, and the conversation shifted.

While the conversation had turned to lighter subjects, more tea and cakes were brought in. Charlotte and Maria began to work at filling everyone's tea while Sir William tried to engage in conversation with Mr. Darcy, and the Colonel remained by me.

Though I wished to speak with Mr. Darcy, I was still suited with this arrangement. The Colonel was engaging, and I simply enjoyed his company.

"Also," Colonel Fitzwilliam added, "when coming into Kent, I was delighted to find that you were among the company. Between you, Mrs. Collins and Miss Maria, I believe that the days shall pass here with delight."

"You flatter us, and I worry that I shall not live up to your expectations."

"You already have lived up to them." He grinned. "My aunt talks a great deal, but I have known her all my life. You and I are strangers, and therefore, we both must render each other as fascinating because there is so little that we already know about each other. Also, Darcy rarely talks when he's here, though he's lively whenever he is at Pemberly. Also, no one at Rosings sings, plays music, or enjoys a dance. However, I have it upon good authority that you play and sing."

"I do, but only a mere little, and that is not spoken by false modesty. With what you are used to hearing, I would pale in comparison."

"You do yourself an injustice. Besides, any sort of amusement would be a diversion, therefore, I promise to be happy with your skills, which I suspect are better than you let on."

"You speak true, cousin," Mr. Darcy voiced suddenly. We all turned to him, as he was just about to sip his tea. "For I have had the pleasure of hearing you sing, Miss Bennet. Do you not recall, Mrs. Collins, when I saw you and Miss Bennet perform together at Lucas Lodge?"

"I do indeed, sir," Charlotte grinned, "and I practically had to drag Lizzy to the pianoforte."

"Internally, I was kicking and screaming all the way," I concurred. "And, from what I hear of the legendary Miss Darcy, I must have brought you great agony, Mr. Darcy."

"No one who heard you could have found anything wanting in your performance. You both were a delight to hear."

This compliment, so frankly bestowed on us, made Charlotte and I blush—for some reason, we felt embarrassed.

"Thank you, Mr. Darcy," Charlotte responded.

"Yes—yes," I stuttered, "thank you, Mr. Darcy."

Colonel Fitzwilliam and Mr. Darcy soon ended their visit and returned to Rosings Park.

When gone, I had more time to reflect on my letters again. With Mr. Wickham, it was amazing how quickly the news on his side became less potent to me. This made it even more apparent to myself that I felt affection for him, but it perhaps was not love.

With Jane's letter, I recalled Miss Bingley's cold visit. If I was to get any answers, I had to get Mr. Darcy alone once more. Unfortunately, I did not see how that could be accomplished.

The next day came, and we found ourselves walking to Rosings Park once more. Upon arrival, I was content in finding that there was more company there than just Lady Catherine and the others. There were a couple of reverends and vicars among the company, as well as some of the other neighbors.

We were introduced, and we all sat down to dinner. Afterward, the men parted, and we women were left to speak with each other. Though there were around eleven women in the room, Lady Catherine was still the one who spoke the most. The rest of us mostly sat there, expecting to only make a response when Lady Catherine wished for someone to speak.

"I must ask," I whispered to Mrs. Jenkinson, "what are all these clergymen doing here?"

"They are candidates," Mrs. Jenkinson responded, "for the options of the new reverend that is to take the late Mr. Collin's place here at Hunsford Parsonage."

"Oh," I said, happy to know the answer for this larger party.

"Miss Maria," Lady Catherine said, "since your sister has been married, have you enjoyed your time in being out and into society?"

"Oh," Maria rushed out, immediately perplexed and afraid to speak, "well, I…"

"My sister was out before I wed," Charlotte Lucas explained.

"That is very unorthodox," Lady Catherine responded.

"How so, madam?" I asked.

"What a strange question. I refer to the fact that the younger sister is out before the eldest got married."

"Oh."

"What else did you assume that I meant? But wait," she looked on me most pointedly. "But you have four sisters, and you are the second eldest?"

"Yes, that is so."

"Are any of your sisters out?"

"Yes, ma'am, all of them are out."

"All five out at once?"

"Is your elder sister married, at least?" One of the other women, named Miss Cheltern, had asked.

"No, she is not."

Charlotte, Mrs. Jenkinson, Anne de Bourgh and Maria were not alarmed by this, but the rest of the women in the room did not know where to look.

"All five sisters out at once," Lady Catherine repeated, flummoxed. "The youngest out before the eldest are married. I have never heard of such a thing. Your younger sister must be very young."

"Yes, ma'am. She is soon to be seventeen."

Lady Catherine still looked alarmed by this.

"She is quite young to be out much in company," I allowed, "but really, I think it would be very hard on younger sisters to not be out in society just because the elder sisters have not the means or inclination to marry early. It would hardly encourage sisterly affection."

"Once more, you speak your opinion very decidedly. It is an uncommon thing."

"Do I have your leave to take that as a compliment, madam?"

"Take it as you will. For I know not what to do with it."

I suppressed a smile.

Soon afterward, the men returned to join the ladies. Due to the volume of guests, many of them single women, Colonel Fitzwilliam found himself to be quite the social creature.

A couple of the women in the company sat near him and engaged him in conversation, and I was not upset by this. Rather, I sat there, wishing to observe everyone and wondering.

As I looked over them all, my eyes scanned the room. When doing so, they accidentally fell on Mr. Darcy. I was surprised when I found that he had been staring directly at me.

I smiled, nodded to him, and he took that as encouragement. Standing up, he crossed the room and sat down next to me. Secretly, I was overjoyed. This was precisely what I would have wished.

"Do not take my cousin's lack of attention to you too personally," Mr. Darcy said, gesturing to Colonel Fitzwilliam. "He is a very social sort of creature."

"What?" I asked, confused at why he said that. Then I gathered his meaning, and I chuckled. "Oh, thank you for the warning, but I was not missing his company."

"You were not? People love Richard."

"Oh, I like him. That must be rightly understood, and I am glad when we speak. But it is in a friendly sort of fashion. And a friend can always speak with others. I am not the sort to expect your cousin to spend his time talking with me when there is much more pleasant company about. But I gather that he prefers the company of women. Am I wrong? You can tell me, for I am not the sort to label him a rattle for being attentive to us."

"Richard and I are similar in one way."

"And what is that?"

"We find women to be intoxicating. To the point where a woman's beauty can overwhelm us."

"Really? I had not the slightest notion that you and he were the sort to be that way. Well, I can believe it of him, but not you."

"And why not me?"

"Because you seem to be cold towards us. Sometimes it seems as if you hold us in disdain. How am I to translate adoration from that?"

"And that is where my cousin and I differ. He has the talent of displaying it in a more outward fashion. With me, my emotions run more internally."

"To the point where they are invisible."

"Are you attempting to willfully misunderstand me then? For I am not afraid of you."

"Have I offended you?"

"A bit."

"And what's an offense between two people who have spent their acquaintance with giving offense to the other? There is a freedom about how we are. Let us not rob each other of that comfort. But if your nature is passionate, then you have never shown it. I can comprehend why, for we live in times that award disinterestedness, but you cannot blame me for seeing what you have never shown."

"Very well," he gave way, "I promise that I shall show my more inward emotions to you always."

"You do not have to if it makes you feel uncomfortable," I added, realizing that I may have been pushing him in a direction that he did not feel comfortable in going. "I do not rule over you, and I have no right to."

"Thank you, but as I said before, I am not afraid of you. Therefore, what I say and do now is me being courageous rather than obeying your whims."

"Very well. But I must assure you that if I gave off any feelings of partiality towards the Colonel, then I was merely being friendly and no more. He was being kind to me, and I was returning his politeness. This is the sad state of the world, is it not? If you are kind and open to them, then it makes you exposed to gossip and people's assumptions. Yet, if you are reserved and spiritless, you may be able to boast of not exposing anything, but no one ever knows what you feel."

"So, it sounds like you and I are on two different sides of a situation, but we are the same for that reason."

"We neither of us perform to strangers, I suppose," I admitted.

Happy that our conversation was going so very well, I wanted to make my stance doubly certain that I was impartial to Colonel Fitzwilliam. The last thing I needed was Mr. Darcy thinking I was trying to ensnare his cousin.

"And," Mr. Darcy continued, "my cousin has the misfortune to not be the firstborn in the family, as you know."

"I gathered that fact when I saw he was a man with a profession. Therefore, you must give me credit in that I can deduce that much, at least."

"I do not mean to trivialize your intelligence. I know you to be smart. It is just that where the Colonel and I are similar in one way, we are dissimilar in another. He cannot marry who he chooses."

Biting my lip, I stared ahead. Was Mr. Darcy thinking of me when he said this? It felt as if he was trying to put me on my guard and make doubly sure that I had no expectations in that quarter.

"With a man such as him," I continued, "what would be the price of an Earl's son? I can only assume that less than fifty thousand pounds would be insufficient for his fiancée's dowry?"

"Fifty thousand is the price that he sets his sight on."

I looked on Colonel Fitzwilliam and was surprised at this.

"I suppose that the entire world is a fortune hunter," I sighed, "and have no choice but to be. Yet the world is also a hypocrite. It encourages us to marry well, but then it labels your actions mercenary if you do. This would not be so very terrible if we ladies also had the right to work as well."

"You are suggesting that you all should have an occupation?"

"I know that the idea scandalizes you."

"Perhaps it does."

"But think of it. If we ladies were allowed to have a profession, then we could bring income into the household. We could, therefore, lean more towards the inclination of marrying gentlemen for love. And you could marry us for love as well."

"Your prescription for our predicament is a sound one, but from selfish reasons—I confess they are selfish—but I am happy, that when I choose a wife, her income is not something I have to worry over."

"I thought that your wife was chosen for you already." I gestured to Anne de Bourgh.

"I make my own fate," he stated boldly, "and I choose the woman that I choose. And when I do, it will be because of the passion that I feel towards her. That, I promise, Miss Bennet."

His dark eyes were intense as he stared at me. I returned his stare with one of my own. This boded well, for if he was of this belief, then maybe I could convince him to think kinder toward Jane's predicament.

"Perhaps that is why you and Mr. Bingley are friends. He seems to be of the sort who would choose for passion as well."

This broke the spell.

Mr. Darcy flinched, and he looked away from me.

"Perhaps he is," he agreed.

"Then why did he leave my sister's side so abruptly after the Netherfield ball?"

My sudden confrontation on this subject clearly alarmed him, but I was not going to give up.

"You do not need to fear me, Mr. Darcy," I whispered, "for you should know by now I bring no danger with you telling me things. I know that Mr. Bingley was partial to my sister, perhaps even as much as she was in love with him."

"She is in love with him?" he asked, surprised by this.

"Well, yes," I stuttered. I did not even understand why he needed to ask the question. "Of course, she is. You recall when Sir William spoke of it. I wish that he had not made his knowledge so public, but it was no less public than when my mother spoke of it, so he was not doing any more harm than she. It is just...my sister is in town, and she has not happened to see Mr. Bingley either. She does not speak of it, but I know her. Her heart is clearly broken over it, and I feel as if I cannot rest until I help her in some way. Mr. Darcy, before you feel overwhelmed with me breaching propriety by speaking like this, then think! If she were your sister, would you believe in any other way than I do now? Also, my father has just died, sir. I realized that what do I have to be afraid of by talking frankly about these sorts of things? The loss of my father has put things into sharper focus."

"Bingley chooses to do as he wishes."

"I do not believe that he does. I believe that somehow, he is being influenced into not loving my sister. I thought that I would ask you because he trusts you. Tell me, did I see everything wrong? Did your friend not love my sister, after all? And we all just saw it incorrectly?"

Darcy did not answer, and I realized that perhaps I had gone too far.

"You do not need to answer that question," I pressed, "I shall not force you to break your friend's confidence. Forgive me for that. But I tell you this because I want to believe that you do not feel animosity towards me any longer. I trust you enough for you to understand that my sister is heartbroken, and I will do everything that I can to help her find her way back to happiness again."

"What do you mean that I once held you in animosity?" he asked.

"I refer to the fact that you did not hold me in a high regard when we met. You could not even bear to be in my presence, of course. But has your opinion changed? I want to believe that we are at least friendly acquaintances now."

"I never despised you, Miss Bennet."

"You did not wish to even dance with me when we first met. If you did not despise me," I grinned, "then you had a funny way of showing it."

"If we were to be set upon to dance now at a ball, then I would rectify the mistake I made, and I would dance with you. Besides, I rectified that mistake when we danced at Netherfield."

"See?" I chuckled, "we are friendly acquaintances now. So, as a friend, do not begrudge me my feelings. She is my sister, and I have a right to care about her happiness."

Mr. Darcy opened his mouth to speak again, but Lady Catherine called out to him.

Our *tête-à-tête* was at an end.

CHAPTER 12

HIS SECRET SOUL

When all the guests were gone and Mr. Darcy was able to return to his bed, he entered, his valet undressed him, and he prepared for slumber.

After the dinner, he had recommended to Lady Catherine what the best choices would be for the new reverend at Hunsford. In truth, his heart was not that much into doing the duty, but he had heard enough good reports of one reverend to know that he would do the service credibly.

But now that he was alone, he sat down at the window and stared out at the moon.

Closing his eyes, he recalled every moment that he had seen and spoken to Elizabeth. She was a beauty, that could not be denied, but everything about her called out to him that evening. After all these months, he could declare her as one of the most handsome women of his acquaintance.

Yet, what sparked so much of his desire for her was her charm, her charisma, her character, and the conversations that they often had with each other.

Tonight, however, was a night unlike any other. The way she spoke with him made it feel as if they had been weaving a tapestry with their words.

Until she had spoken of Mr. Bingley! That was the only part of the conversation he did not recall with a favorable eye. She claimed that Jane had loved Mr. Bingley after all. From what he had observed, Jane never showed any particular regard for Bingley, but Elizabeth would know better than him, surely. Also, how was Jane's reserved nature any different than his? For now, he realized Elizabeth had felt that he despised her, but it was not so. Did he take a step too far somewhere?

However, he soon dismissed this notion from his mind. He was in love with Elizabeth, but there was the chance she had been looking at Jane with a partiality that siblings often had for each other. Therefore, perhaps she was not the most objective judge.

Despite this acknowledgment, Darcy knew he was being a hypocrite. He had advised Bingley to not pursue Jane Bennet. Even at Canter's Abbey, he still had to press his will on Bingley.

Therefore, now to be pursuing her younger sister would look horrible of him. Would Bingley even be able to face him again? Sadly, that was a conflict that he would have to face when the option presented itself.

For now, he was resolute. He knew that there was no other way to satisfy himself. He had to have her. He had to marry her. There was nothing for it now because he was completely in her power. Everything about her moved him.

Also, that evening, he had made his feelings for her too marked to be mistaken.

At the soonest opportunity, he would marry her. Also, she had professed as much that she had heard of his aunt's desires for him to marry Anne. That was perhaps something that was keeping her from thinking he could have any real designs on her. He would destroy any impediment to their marriage and calm any doubts in her mind of she not being an option to him.

All that he required now was the opportunity to ask her. He did not wish to do it where there was the possibility of any sort of company coming upon them.

Rather, he wished to have her alone, all to himself, where they could enjoy the intimacy of the moment. At that particular moment, he let his dreams get ahead of him as he envisioned Elizabeth walking across the grass toward Rosings. Like the mirage that she was, she disappeared immediately.

Leaning back in his seat, Darcy rubbed his eyes, and then he snuffed out the candle.

Getting into his bed, he closed his eyes, but only to not fall asleep immediately. Rather, his imagination was at Hunsford Parsonage, where Elizabeth was waiting for him, in his secret soul.

Rolling over, his imagination overwhelmed him, and he imagined Elizabeth on the other end of his bed…

"Mr. Darcy, good evening," She smiled, and her eyes twinkled in the moonlight.

Quickly, Darcy jumped out of the bed and moved towards her.

"Elizabeth," he sighed, "if you come, then you come to stay."

"I am not afraid of you," she responded, "we say that to each other a great deal, do we not?"

"Yes, we do. But fear me, you must. There is no likelihood that I am able to control myself now."

"You shall propose to me tomorrow," she whispered, arching her eyebrows in the process, "therefore, am I not your wife tonight already?"

Looking down on her with an intense desire in his eyes, he felt his resolve slipping away.

"You are," he responded, his voice raspy, "and now, prepare yourself."

Leaning down, he kissed her savagely. Feeling her lips upon his was intoxicating, and he could now release all self-restraint and allow his control to diminish.

He had her for a wife!

He needed nothing else in this moment.

"Turn around, dearest," he whispered harshly and desperately. "Turn around for me."

Elizabeth turned around, and Mr. Darcy slowly began to remove all the pins from her hair. Soon her hair fell down to the sides of her face, falling free. Leaning down, Mr. Darcy ran his hands through her hair and kissed her neck.

Closing her eyes, Elizabeth let out a sigh as she felt the tenderness of his lips upon her skin.

"Forgive me," he gasped, "but let no impediment find me now. I no longer fear anything."

Lowering his hands down, he began to unfasten her dress, where it fell to the floor.

"Give me leave to continue," he requested.

"I accept you," she responded.

"Love me, Elizabeth. Love me always."

Quickly, he yanked her undergarments from off her. Next, he lifted her up and kissed her passionately.

"Tell me that you love me," he whispered.

"I love you."

"Tell me that you do not care for my cousin, or for any other man but myself!"

"I shall never love anyone else."

Darcy laid her on the bed, and he looked on her, bare and beautiful before him. The light of the moon fell through the windows and lit up her gorgeous skin.

Slowly, Darcy removed his nightshirt, and he leaned over her.

First, he ran his hands from the bottom of her legs, up to her thighs, over her stomach, and finally, he reached her breasts. Elizabeth closed her eyes as she became eclipsed by the feelings of his fingers running over her nipples repeatedly. Rolling her head over, she dug her mouth into the pillows to stifle her sound.

"No," Darcy dissuaded her, "I want to hear your cries for me. Look up, Elizabeth. Let me see your fine eyes as I make you content."

Obeying, Elizabeth looked up once more, and her cries of happiness escaped her as Darcy lowered his head, closed his mouth around her breasts, and began to kiss her most ardently.

To feel the softness of her flesh within his mouth, Darcy felt himself come closer to achieving what he felt would always be rightfully his.

Repeatedly he caressed her nipples in between his teeth and fingers, overwhelmed with achieving his desires at last.

Then he kissed her lips once more as he felt her hands slide down his back, grabbing his bottom and holding onto him desperately.

To feel her passion for him grow bolder was everything that was pleasing for him.

He was in love with her.

She was in love with him.

And no longer was he to labor under propriety and the expectations of the outside world.

To make her more at ease, he lowered his hand down along her stomach and closed his fingers between her thighs.

"I want you to feel no pain when I enter you," he informed her. "Never fear, this shall help."

When doing so, Darcy took his time, slowly rocking Elizabeth back and forth from within. Her eyes closed as her breath escaped her. Moaning out, she grabbed the sheets as Darcy marveled at her. He was the first and only man who could produce such sensations within her, and he found her helplessness at his hands as intoxicating. She was prepared. She was content, and he was the one who claimed her.

She was his.

And she would belong only to him.

Rolling on top of her, Darcy wrapped her legs around his hips and welcomed the sensation of falling into her...

Opening his eyes again, Darcy blinked.

He had forced himself out of his daydream before it had gotten too far ahead of him.

Often his dreams of Elizabeth only went as far as kissing her, feeling the warmth and softness of her lips pressed against his.

Yet now, it had gone so very far, so very deep, that he also dreamt of her fully becoming his.

He knew where the source of his realizing his full desires came from. It was his cousin. Colonel Fitzwilliam's marked attentions to Elizabeth forced him to confront the reality that had been growing within him.

He was in love with Elizabeth Bennet, yes.

But now, that love could not be denied or overcome. It was a passion that ran so deep his blood would boil at the thought of any other man winning her affections.

Therefore, his decision was now made for him.

"Bingley," he whispered to himself, "please forgive me. Everyone, forgive me. But I have no choice now." Looking at the ceiling, he saw Elizabeth Bennet before him, and he offered up the last of his pleas to her. "Elizabeth, we shall be married soon. For my sake, be kind to me. Because I am entirely within your power."

He would propose to her. Now he just needed to wait for the right time and the opportunity. But he was determined. He would find it.

CHAPTER 13

IGNORANCE IS BLISS

*M*y time at Rosings Park was filled with all the expected joys that could come along with being near a great estate that had extensive grounds; I grew to love the land, even if I did not love all the people who lived on it.

Getting my bonnet on, I decided to go for my daily walk along the woods and hills of Hunsford. At this point, I had discovered many pleasant walks and much to see, for there was much to admire there.

However, as I had done so, I walked past the sitting room in the parsonage, and for some reason, I recalled when Mr. Collins had proposed to me the night after the Netherfield ball.

Tying my bonnet, the scene occurred very vividly within my mind...

I had been sitting with my mother and Kitty, speaking of the casual nonsense that one usually does speak about after a ball, when Mr. Collins had entered and approached my mother—while referring to me.

"May I hope, madam, for your interest with your fair daughter Elizabeth, when I solicit for the honor of a private audience with her in the course of this morning?" he asked her.

When hearing this, I felt my blood rise, surprised and mortified.

What I would have given for my mother to not accept this request, but I knew that was a vain wish. She agreed immediately and hastened Kitty to follow her out of the room. But I was not prepared to give up without fighting for them to remain.

"Mama," I pleaded, "do not go. I beg you will not go. Mr. Collins must excuse me. He can have nothing to say to me that anybody need not hear. I am going away myself."

"No, no, nonsense, Lizzy," she argued, "I desire you to stay where you are." Every feeling within me forbid it! As such, I prepared myself to rush out of the door when our mother barred my path. "Lizzy, I *insist* upon your staying and hearing Mr. Collins."

It was too direct a command; I could not disobey. Kitty gave me one last fleeting look, and then she followed my mother out while I sat down, awaiting my fate where I would have to hear an offer I never desired to have. Mr. Collins walked towards me, removed a flower from one of the vases—stumbling in the process—and then set the flower down in front of me.

"Believe me," he had begun, "my dear Miss Elizabeth, that your modesty, so far from doing you any disservice, rather adds to your other perfections. You would have been less amiable in my eyes had there *not* been this little unwillingness, but allow me to assure you, that I have your respected mother's permission for this address. You can hardly doubt the purport of my discourse. However, your natural delicacy may lead you to dissemble, my attentions have been too marked to be mistaken. Almost as soon as I entered the house, I singled you out as the companion of my future life. But before I am run away with by my feelings on this subject, perhaps it would be advisable for me to state my reasons for marrying—and, moreover, for coming into Hertfordshire with the design of selecting a wife, as I certainly did."

I shall never deny that I almost laughed at this declaration. I could not imagine Mr. Collins, who was so very serious in composure and disposition, being run away with his feelings. Fortunately, I need not have worried about it, because Mr. Collins was so preoccupied with his proposal, that he did not even notice my expressions. As cold as it was for me to admit, but I did not sympathize with him. I took no pleasure in hurting his pride or breaking his heart, but my denial was something that was purely out of obligation and for the happiness of both. He was the last man that could make me happy as was I the last woman on earth who could make him so. Yet, he continued, as was his way.

"My reasons for marrying are, first, I think it a right thing for every clergyman in easy circumstances (like myself) to set the example of matrimony in his parish. Secondly, I am convinced that it will add very greatly to my happiness; and thirdly—which perhaps I ought to have mentioned earlier, it is the particular advice and recommendation of the very noble lady whom I have the honor of calling patroness. Twice has she condescended to give me her opinion (unasked too!) on this subject, and it was but the very Saturday night before I left Hunsford—between our pools at quadrille, while Mrs. Jenkinson was arranging Miss de Bourgh's footstool, that she said, 'Mr. Collins, you must marry. A clergyman like you must marry. Choose properly, choose a gentlewoman for *my* sake, and for your *own*, let her be an active, useful sort of person, not brought up high, but able to make a small income go a good way. This is my advice. Find such a woman as soon as you can, bring her to Hunsford, and I will visit her.' Allow me, by the way, to observe, my fair cousin, that I do not reckon the notice and kindness of Lady Catherine de Bourgh as among the least of the advantages in my power to offer."

He continued in this manner, and then he got to the heart of the matter.

"But the fact is, that being, as I am, to inherit this estate after the death of your honored father, I could not satisfy myself without resolving to choose a wife from among his daughters, that the loss to them might be as little as possible, when the melancholy event takes place—which, however, as I have already said, may not be for several years. This has been my motive, my fair cousin, and I flatter myself it will not sink me in your esteem. And now nothing remains for me but to assure you in the most animated language of the violence of my affection."

Soon, he also began to speak of his being indifferent to my small dowry, and then he settled on our happiness as a couple. And that was when I knew I had no choice but to stop him and bring an end to all his dreams.

"You are too hasty, sir," I cried. "You forget that I have made no answer. Let me do it without further loss of time. Accept my thanks for the compliment you are paying me. I am very sensible of the honor of your proposals, but it is impossible for me to do otherwise than to decline them."

My reaction was met with denial on his part, of refusal to take my words seriously, and then I had to race out of the room for my declining his offer to take me seriously. My mother would not forgive me, and my father was the one who had taken my side.

My father!

The memory of his kindness to me had come rushing back to me, and I felt my heart soften immediately. His face being within my mind had forced me to fall out of my daydreams and feel the bitterness of reality.

Suddenly, I was come upon by Charlotte, and her presence had forced me to distance myself from my daydreams even more.

"Lizzy, are you well?" she asked me.

"Yes, I am. Do I not look in good health?"

"Well, you do look somewhat flushed."

"Then it is a sign that it is nothing that a little fresh air will not cure. I am going for my daily walk, for I daresay I have grown to love these woods and hills as you have."

Charlotte smiled, and we exchanged glances.

I was the one who your late husband had proposed to, I had thought in that moment. It was an ungenerous thought, but it was no more unnatural than what she had thought when she had accepted his proposal to her. She and I were the same sort of imperfection, therefore. As a result, I had nothing to be ashamed of.

Nodding to her, I went off to haunt my daily pathway.

Running my hand along a tree trunk, I found the peace that comes with solitude and not being confined indoors. I was outside, and if there were no one in sight, I would then be free to find the liberty I always enjoyed—I could run.

Looking around, I saw no one, so I looked forward and began to run through the woods and along the grass. Next, I reached a slight hill, and I felt my spirit rise up, and sweet liberty was within my grasp. Raising up my arms, I ran down the hill, feeling the breeze blow around me.

"You are like a sprite then," I heard someone shout behind me. Alarmed at the disturbance, while also being embarrassed at being discovered, I turned around sharply and discovered it was Colonel Fitzwilliam.

Upon seeing him, my spirits no longer were disturbed. For if there was anyone who would understand, it was him.

"And a sprite I will no longer remain if you reveal my secret to the world," I responded, remaining still and folding my hands in front of me. "Can you keep my secret?"

"With pleasure," he responded, tipping his hat to me. "I find you to be on marvelous display now."

"Thank you," I said, "I do it to settle my spirits whenever they get too high. Will you judge me to no longer be a lady?"

"A true lady has more uniqueness to her than always being confined to a drawing room. You are precisely as you ought to be."

"Then you give me leave to still be Elizabeth Bennet?"

"I would prefer it if you were no one else but who you are now." I smiled.

"I am making my customary walk whenever I visit the park. Would you be willing to take this turn with me?"

"With pleasure."

We both turned and walked along, enjoying the scenery.

"So, you like to walk as well?" I asked.

"My aunt's home has lovely landscape around it. I find that seeing woods and hills can improve the soul."

"I agree."

"By the way, forgive me for reminding you of sadder times, but I heard about your father. I am sorry about that."

"Thank you. And with you, you have the good pleasure of your parents remaining alive. Cherish it, Colonel, for you have only one set of parents. And they do not live forever, despite what you tell yourself."

"Yes, we do have the tendency to think they are immortal. You and Darcy are similar in that way. I felt pain for him when he lost his father as well. One is never the same again, I gather."

"No, one is not. And for Miss Darcy, she must have it harder as well when losing her father."

"She, fortunately, has Darcy and me as her guardians. We may not be her father, but we try to supply the substitute."

"You also are Miss Darcy's guardian?"

"Yes. Darcy does not have to do it alone. But he does his best to be the father that she has lost. Yet he has experience with being a patriarchal character, despite being a young man. He is often the paternal side of every friendship that he has with his friends."

"Yes, I saw that same habit and manner with a friend of his, Mr. Bingley."

"Ah, you know Bingley?"

"Yes, I do. And by the sound of your voice, you know him as well."

"Yes, I do, indeed. Bingley is a pleasant and gentlemanlike man. He's a very good friend of Darcy's."

"Yes, I have often seen how much of bosom friends that they are. Darcy does not seem like the sort of man who bestows his good opinion on anyone, so it shows how special Bingley is to him."

"Yes, that is very true. But very little is deserving of Darcy's care. That is why he is still single now, I suppose. I have met very few in the world who are worthy of him."

"You think very well of your cousin."

"He has been there for me, as a friend and as a financier. As you can imagine, being born a younger son, I have not always had the financial liberties that my elder brother has had. Therefore, I regret so very much to admit this, but Darcy has helped me at times. In many ways, he has been like an extended brother towards me. That is perhaps the main reason he and I share a dual guardianship with his sister. Our situations have often led to us being together as two brothers where we both stabilized each other."

"I have heard many different accounts of Mr. Darcy's character, to the point where I am always confused."

"If you are regarding the fact that some call him proud or throw some other charge at his feet, then recall this maxim I often live by and justify my own actions towards: beware of men and women who have *no* enemies, for that means either they do not care strongly about anything, or they hide their evil in ways that are truly terrifying."

"The demon underneath."

"Like so."

"Well, that is a very sound bit of advice, but I shall still trust to my own will and counsel about what I believe and how I measure a man. For, too often I have been given advice, and it did not work on every occasion."

"Do as you will," he smiled at me, "for I dare not ever take away from a lady her right to make up her own mind."

"Oh, you are so very generous," I teased.

"May I always be so," he teased in return.

As we walked along, I did not wish to end the discussion on Mr. Darcy. Whether my feelings for him fell towards the positive or negative in that particular moment, the man was an enigma. He was something to be wondered at, marveled at, and sometimes repulsed by, to the point where he was, and forever would be, a fascination. Therefore, I did desire to glean more about his character, and Colonel Fitzwilliam was just the sort to give me all the answers that I needed.

"When in regards to assisting you," I continued, "I am assuming that you mean more than just financially? Do you rely upon his advice in the same manner that part of me just relied on yours?"

"Yes. For once, he did persuade me out of making a most imprudent match."

"He persuaded you not to marry someone?"

"Yes, and he was correct, for it was not the wisest thing to do. The woman was marrying me for my title and not because she loved me. Yes, being a second son, I do have to marry well, but I still desire for there to be some affection in the case. I met one woman of a wealthy family, and I truly did enjoy her. I doted on her terribly. But she wanted to marry the son of an earl. Yes, I did consider her for wealth, but I did more than just that. She wanted to marry me solely for my name. Darcy helped me see that her love for me was nonexistent and that I was simply seeing what I wished to see."

"How did he reveal that?"

"He placed himself in her way, offering her attentions where I would overhear them. Once I was not in her presence, and he was bestowing his polite words unto her, she clearly shifted her attentions toward him. She did not want me. She wanted a prize."

"But you desire wealth yourself."

"But I promise, I do desire affection in the case as well. Darcy had staged it all so that I would see the true person that she was, and he was right."

"Have you loved since?"

"No, for you know not the pain that situation caused me. After a circumstance such as that, it is hard to trust again. I let my affection for her blind me into seeing what I wanted to see and not what was there."

"How did Mr. Darcy see that she did not care for you?"

"He said that she received my attentions with complacency and not true regard. I took her behavior for demureness, or an attempt to hide that she was enraptured by me, ugly mortal that I am. After all, some women are trained to conceal their affection so that they are not exposed to the world's derision for not being too careful. I never liked that practice, but my personal taste is perverse, I suppose. However, Darcy claimed that if she cared for me, then there would be more outward regard. He was correct. Love is a frightening thing. When it all works, it is beautiful. Yet, when it deceives us, we are never the same again."

"I am heartily sorry for you, Colonel. Very rarely do I hear men speak of their losses when it comes to heartache."

"Because we are not allowed to speak of them. As, perhaps, you are not either. For, we are in a time where, if it is not pleasant to speak of, then it is not spoken about. But I cannot complain, for I have been spared an attachment where there was not much affection in the case on her side. Yes, Darcy has taken care of me, as he does with Bingley in the same manner."

My ears perked up at this.

"What do you mean in the same manner?" I asked.

"Well, as I understand it, he persuaded Bingley out of the prospect of making the wrong choice when it came to marriage."

"Was Mr. Bingley interested in a woman who his friend found to be imprudent?"

"Yes. Well, I am assuming. In truth, I ought not to have made so bold a declaration, because I know none of the particulars. He spoke of a friend of his that he persuaded out of marrying the wrong sort of girl, but he never gave a name. The only reason that I assumed it was Bingley was because he had just left Bingley's company. But I could be in error."

"Did Mr. Darcy give any reason for this interference?"

"I believe there were some very strong objections to the lady."

"What objections? Did she lack fortune?"

"I know not the particulars of the case."

Alarm and resentment overcame me. I knew that Mr. Darcy had been concealing things from me, but I was not aware that it was to this extent. These revelations had a contradictory effect on me. Part of me was shocked and in pain to hear it, yet it also was beneficial that I had learned of it all. However, this agony apparently was displayed all over my face because the Colonel had seen it.

"Miss Bennet, are you unwell?" he asked.

"Yes. I just am disturbed, is all. I just do not understand what right that Mr. Darcy had deciding in what manner his friend was to be happy. Why was it his right and power to be the judge?"

"You do not praise his interference?"

"I cannot when I do not know the particulars of the situation. Yet, if there was not much affection between the two of them, then perhaps I could concede to his better judgment, but therein is the crisis, I do not know the particulars. Therefore, I cannot declare that Mr. Darcy was an angel in this situation, protecting his friend in the proper manner. There is such a thing, after all, as over-persuasion. And sometimes it can cause more trouble than it does solve anything."

"If that be so, then it lessens the triumph of my cousin a great deal, I do not deny."

"Yes, it would."

In that moment, I knew that I was not fully governor of my

sentiments and thoughts. Something was bound to betray me. Therefore, I had nothing else to do but to untangle myself from Colonel Fitzwilliam's company and be free of him. It mattered not anyway! His good or bad opinion of me would have no sway over any of my actions.

"Forgive me, but I feel a sudden headache come over me," I excused, "may I have leave to return to the parsonage?"

"Would you mind if I escorted you on the way back?" he asked.

"With pleasure," I said. Arm in arm, we returned to the parsonage, and when I was left alone, I found the safety of my solitude.

Mr. Bingley had been willing to make Jane an offer.

Darcy was indeed the one who had separated them.

I could never forgive him.

CHAPTER 14

THE PAINS OF CONFRONTATION

The next day, we received a letter inviting us to Rosings Park again to dine with them and to play a set of cards. My heart was not into it at all, and I begged Charlotte would excuse me from the company.

"I would never press you," she declared, "and if you want, I can remain home with you and brave Lady Catherine's displeasure."

"Oh, Charlotte, do not say such a thing," Sir William protested.

"Father, you sound like my late husband," Charlotte responded, "and that is not a good thing."

"Thank you, Charlotte," I responded, "however, you need not remain from the festivities on my account. I shall recover faster in peace and in solitude."

She, Maria and Sir William went away to Rosings, while I could receive considerable time away from Mr. Darcy, the Colonel, their intrusive aunt and their lifeless cousin, Anne. I needed time to recover and find a way to subdue my spirits. If I were to face Mr. Darcy again, it would be in a calm manner where I would find a way to reveal what I had learned and not unleash my wrath upon him. Nothing could be gained from not controlling my anger. However, at the moment, I knew I could not trust myself. I was enraged, and I hated him. I was not likely capable of any truly impartial behavior, as I was overcome with my sensibility. Whatever I felt, I felt it to the extreme.

As I sat there, in my bedroom, I felt the walls closing in. I felt cramped and confined.

I was tired of being confined and restricted by things! Too much of life was restraint that was needless and oppressive for no reason.

I wanted to be out and running around. I had to be out!

Putting on my coat, gloves, bonnet and scarf, I told one of the servants where I was headed, and I set out for one of the familiar walks that I had along the parsonage.

Through the woods and along the hills, I rambled. And when no one else was in sight, I picked up speed and began to run through the hills. When exhausted, I fell down on the ground, laying amongst the grass, and I stretched my arms out.

"Father," I whispered to the air, "what would you do in my case? Now that I think on it, you would laugh, and perhaps you would find the folly and foolishness of it all. You would not have chosen to act, because this all would have been diverting to you. However, I want to believe, now that your spirit is everywhere and looks down upon us, that you would act differently. Therefore, what should I do? What ought I to do?"

Suddenly, I sensed some movement to my left. Rolling my head, I looked to my left, and it was my turn to jump. Standing a few feet away from me was Mr. Darcy!

"I see that I interrupt your prayer," he began.

"Yes," I jumped up, "you do."

"Wo betide that I interrupt a discussion between father and daughter. If it helps," he added, "sometimes, I speak to my parents as well. Even though they are also gone."

His simple confession to this had quite unnerved and distracted me. For a brief moment, I ceased to recall my purpose for despising him. It was a strange thing. For I was enraged, and yet, seeing him there, speaking of his deceased parents, I could not help but feel sorry for him.

"I comprehend the feeling," I added, "and I am sorry for it. People say that lost loved ones never fully leave us. Yet that is not what I find. They leave and then leave us behind, and we wonder where they are, and how we would be if they had not gone so far away from us."

"Precisely," he said, looking nervous.

"I did not expect to see you."

"I heard of your withholding yourself from the visit to Rosings. Therefore, I came down to the parsonage to inquire after your health. I was told that you were out, so I wandered the area to find you. And we have found each other."

"Yes, we have. You look nervous," I observed.

"Yes, I am. I have a great reason to be overcome with anxiety."

Suddenly, I recalled my purpose.

"Is it because you are speaking to the sister of a woman whose life you ruined?" I inquired.

This sudden attack on his character clearly startled Darcy. I was not afraid, for I felt a desire to get to the heart of the secret that he seemed desirous of keeping. I did not have all the time in the world! Therefore, neither should he.

"I beg your pardon?" he asked.

"You need not pretend to be ignorant of what I speak," I added, resigned. "Let us speak truths now, Darcy." I took a few steps forward and stood in his way. "All this time, I thought you and I were gathering a better acquaintance and learning to comprehend the other. But how could you do it all this time? How could you look on me knowing that you were the man who ruined, perhaps forever, the happiness of my beloved sister?"

Darcy's eyes shifted, and then he turned away from me.

"You separated my sister from your friend, under whatever motive you deemed just and proper, yet neither of these excuses shall satisfy me. Do you deny it, Mr. Darcy?"

At this point, he had been looking away from me, then he wielded on me with coldness.

"I have no wish to deny it. I separated Mr. Bingley from your sister, and I rejoice in my success. You could argue that, until now, I have been kinder to him than towards myself."

I opened my mouth and closed it. He honestly felt no remorse toward his behavior.

"How did you discover this?" he asked.

"It does not matter through what source I discovered it. All that matters is that I did, and you have been hiding things from me."

"Who told you?"

"I shall not tell. For it shows me you are more concerned with who exposed your secret rather than regret for your own actions. You do not even feel a semblance of pain over that agony that you have caused another."

"What I did, I did in the service of being a friend."

"What you did, Mr. Darcy, was separate two young people who loved each other, and now do not even blush under the weight of his own coldness. What was more, when I asked you if you had seen my sister in town, or knew of her being there, you lied to me. You sat before me and lied. I thought deception was not something that you were capable of?"

"It is not."

"You speak one thing and practice another!"

"I simply spared you the truth by not speaking of it, but now that you have pointed it out to me, have I denied it?"

"You speak of telling the truth after lying about it for so long? This is the even-handed dealing of your logic? Now I have every reason in the world to think ill of you. No motive can excuse the unjust and ungenerous part you acted there. You dare not, you cannot deny, that you have been the principal, if not the only means of dividing them from each other—of exposing one to the censure of the world for caprice and instability, and the other to its derision for disappointed hopes, and involving them both in misery of the acutest kind."

"All that I have done was in the service of a friend."

"And what I do now, I do in the service of a sister. And that action is simple: I stand up to you, Mr. Darcy. I do not quake and bow down to your intimidating manner, where all must pay homage to your *superior* intellect. Tell me once and for all, under the part of yourself that claims to have veracity, does Mr. Bingley know that my sister is in town or not? Or, did you conspire against them both in that regard? Did you know of my sister's being in town, and like the Bingley sisters, did you assist them in keeping my sister separated from their brother?"

Mr. Darcy looked down at his feet, his face like stone.

"My eyes are up here, sir," I interjected, "if you would but honor me with looking into them, then I would be most obliged."

"Yes, I did know that your sister was in town," he confirmed.

"And once more, you rejoice in your success."

"As I said, what I did, Miss Bennet, was in the service of a friend. It was done, however, and it was done from the best intention that is within me."

"To act in such a manner and call it propriety, I cannot live under such coldness, and I will not do it. Whatever friendship that you and I have, it is at an end. Though, nothing of this should have ever come as a surprise. I gave you a second chance, but I should have clung to my first impressions. After all, my opinion of you, my disdain for your character, was most decided when your character was unfolded in the recital, which I received many months ago from Mr. Wickham. On this subject, what can you have to say? In what imaginary act of friendship can you here defend yourself? Or under what misrepresentation can you here impose upon others?"

"Mr. Wickham?" he repeated. "Why do you say that name?"

"Because that name helped me understand the cold heart of the man who I am speaking to now."

"You take an eager interest in that gentleman's concerns," he spoke, his eyes firm, his voice tranquil, but his eyes flashing with anger. I had stricken a nerve within him, and I, therefore, rejoiced in my success.

"Who that knows what his misfortunes have been, can help feeling an interest in him?" I questioned.

"His misfortunes!" repeated Darcy, contemptuously. "Yes, his misfortunes have been great indeed."

"And of your infliction," I cried, with energy. "You have reduced him to his present state of poverty—comparative poverty. You have withheld the advantages which you must know to have been designed for him. You have deprived the best years of his life of that independence, which was no less his due than his dessert. You have done all this! And yet you can treat the mention of his misfortune with contempt and ridicule."

"And this," Mr. Darcy voiced, clearly bitter, "is your opinion of me? This is the estimation in which you hold me! I thank you for explaining it so fully." He turned away from me again, took a few steps and rubbed his face down. Next, he turned to me, and the turn of his countenance was something that I would never forget. It was strong, bitter, and for a moment, even I was scared of him. However, I soon recovered from that and returned his glare.

"My faults," he continued, "according to this calculation, are heavy indeed!" Next, he walked up to me and stopped within a few steps.

"But perhaps," he added, "these offenses might have been overlooked, had not your pride been hurt by my honest confession of the scruples that had long prevented my allowing my friend to form any serious design on your sister. These bitter accusations might have been suppressed, had I, with greater policy, concealed my struggles, and flattered your family into the belief of my being impelled by unqualified, unalloyed inclination, by reason, by reflection, by everything. But disguise of every sort is my abhorrence. Nor am I ashamed of the friendship that you and I have gathered together. My desires to separate your sister from my friend were natural and just. Could you expect me to rejoice at him in the inferiority of your family's connections? To congratulate him on the hope of relations, whose condition in life is so decidedly beneath his own?"

My patience could endure no more. My anger rose, my resentment had reached its full height, and I was afraid no longer.

"I will hear no more from you, for your mind and mentality is too inferior for me to consider it with anything else but reproach and contempt. And you are mistaken, Mr. Darcy, in thinking this explanation assisted you, but only it spared me any concern I may have felt in arguing with you, had you behaved in a more gentlemanlike manner."

With this declaration, I saw him flinch, but I continued on.

"From the very beginning—from the first moment, I may almost say—of my acquaintance with you, your manners, impressing me with the fullest belief of your arrogance, your conceit, and your selfish disdain of the feelings of others, were such as to form the groundwork of disapprobation on which succeeding events have built so immovable a dislike, and I had not known you a month before I felt that you were the last man in the world whom I could ever feel any friendly affection for. I tried to make peace between us, and you return my attempts with a deceit that you claim now was not even a part of your character. You claim to be ever so full of integrity, but you cannot even see that you lied to me? A person who cannot see the flaw that they possess is not impervious. They do not own their flaws. But rather, their flaws own them. Your flaws own you. And I do not have to live under such a tyrannical mistake."

"Miss Bennet—"

"Do not say my name!" I roared. "Do not speak my name again, and I will not speak yours. Because our very natures are too different for peace to ever come between us again. Because we are on two sides of a situation that has led me to realize that I can never trust you again. To look someone in the eye, knowing that you hurt their family member, who was guiltless of so many things, and then find faultlessness within yourself where there is truly fault. I cannot get on at all, and never, and I mean never, will my dislike cease for you now. What I believe now is that the person who I have grown to know over these last few days has been a creature of my own imagination. It was not you, Mr. Darcy. You are a shadow, a false thought, and a stranger to me. I do not know you, and I rejoice in saying that I do not wish to. We shall walk away from each other now, and it shall be as if we never knew each other. I can see that, due to my *supposed* inferiority in every manner that you lose nothing by this breach."

"Miss Bennet—"

"I said, do not say my name! Do not call me by such, or anything else. It is my name, and I have the right to cling to it as I may. What walks away from you, Mr. Darcy, is an honest woman. And that shall be the last memories you have of the woman named Bennet."

Irate, I marched off, and then I ran away, for fear of him wishing to pursue me.

Back to Hunsford, I ran. When reaching its doorstep, I ran and saw one of the servants gaping at me.

"Miss Elizabeth?" she asked. "Is something the matter?"

"No," I rushed out, "I just need a moment of peace and solitude."

I raced up the steps, went to my room and fell on the bed. My head was aching under the pains of all that I had learned, and my stomach felt sick under the agony of having to argue with someone.

Arguing is and never shall be something that often allows closure or peace. But rather, even when you are in the right, it can often lead to spirits being disrupted, inner peace becoming roused and more upset—and the worst headache that is imaginable.

I felt the walls close in around me, and I was happy with it. Here was my sanctuary. Here was my haven, and I was safe from everything that was outside. Including Mr. Darcy. Little did I know how incorrect I was.

CHAPTER 15

MR. DARCY REGRETS

At first, Darcy's impulse was to pursue Elizabeth. However, the sight of her running away from him made him fully aware of how much she held him in disdain. And that she was willing to flee him in such an overwhelming manner, hurt his pride and sense of inner security.

Turning around, Darcy marched off, back to Rosings. Upon entering, he found that he was immediately come upon by Lady Catherine, who had been wondering where he had been.

"My apologies, aunt," he rushed out, "but I must attend to something."

"Surely, it can wait, Darcy," Lady Catherine demanded.

"Forgive me, Aunt, but no, it cannot. I just recalled that I have something I need to do. And I would only be a coward if I delayed it any longer."

Changing his mind, Darcy dashed back down the stairs and out the front door. At first, he walked quickly down the road, and then, when meeting the grass, he picked up his pace and began to jog.

Once he got within view of Hunsford, he broke out into a hasty run. If he was lucky, he could arrive and speak to Elizabeth in solitude before Charlotte and her family returned from Rosings.

He had gotten everything all wrong!

First, he had assumed she was aware that he was in love with her. She was not, and it became quite clear that their relationship appeared very different from their points of view.

He had regarded their discussions as playful and sensuous banter.

She had regarded it as disagreeable arguments.

She had discovered that he had done everything to persuade Mr. Bingley to cease his attentions towards her sister.

And she was correct; he had hidden the truth from her. When putting it all plainly, he had lied to her. Therefore, his actions were as clear as the sky. He had been a hypocrite in every manner a person could be so.

While still confused about Jane Bennet's true feelings toward Mr. Bingley, he was certain about one thing: clearly, Mr. Wickham had imposed himself on Elizabeth Bennet, and that he owed her the truth.

"In this," he grunted as he ran, almost out of breath, "you may defend yourself. If you claim to care for her, then protect her, at least."

He was in agony and did not know what he was going to say, nor how he was going to convey himself. For indeed, he had never committed to such rash action before in his life. He felt as if he was running toward a cliff now, and there was no way that his will would lessen. Therefore, if his spirit was to peradventure half a league ahead into the abyss that was irrationality, then he might as well go the rest of the distance.

For so long, he did what was correct, and perhaps now the only thing that could be done was to be incorrect. Maybe, in such cases, impropriety was the answer. Darcy was not aware at the time, but he was slightly crazed, driven to the very depths of temporary madness that disappointed affections could cause. He was a man undone.

Inwardly, he knew that nothing could be gained by simply fading away from her. He had to make her aware of his side of things. Perhaps, in his emotional state, he was wishing to obtain the two things that all of us humans try to gain when being forsaken: obtaining closure and also getting the final word in.

All he knew was that he needed to see her one last time.

Once more, he found himself ringing the doorbell to Hunsford parsonage. When it was answered by a servant, he inquired to know if anyone was at home.

"Mrs. Collins, her father and sister are still dining at Rosings," the servant reported, "and the only occupant at home is Miss Bennet."

"Very good," Darcy said, his tone hurried, for every moment felt like a weight. If he did not see her soon, then he would lose his resolve.

"May you tell her that I shall be in the sitting room, awaiting her company if she would be so good as to join me."

Darcy dashed into the house without waiting to be invited.

"Yes, sir," the servant responded, a little wary. The servant went upstairs, and Darcy began to pace back and forth. His nerves were too rattled for him to sit down.

Soon, the servant returned, looking red in the face.

"I am sorry, sir," she informed him, "but the lady says that she is unwell and cannot be seen at this time."

Darcy opened his mouth, closed it, and then opened it again. Only to close it once more. If he were to act on his impulses, then he would become the subject of gossip in the county, and that was the last thing that he wanted. Despite knowing this, he was too compelled, and his impulses had quite overtaken him.

"Then I am sorry for what is about to occur," he stated strongly, but slowly. "I shall need you as the chaperone for this situation."

"Chaperone?"

"Yes."

Suddenly, he rushed up the steps.

"But, sir!" the servant called.

As Darcy reached the steps, he turned back to her.

"Madam," he began, "you must follow me. Recall that you are my chaperone."

The poor servant was perplexed and shocked. However, to do her duty well and see to it that Miss Elizabeth Bennet was not alone while this man appeared to be quite bewildered, she followed anyway. She was a slight thing and did not know what she could do if Mr. Darcy would prove to do anything ungentlemanlike. Yet, she would have to try.

Reaching the second floor, where the bedrooms were, Darcy turned back to the servant.

"Which one is Miss Bennet's room?" he inquired. The servant did not respond.

"Julia?" Elizabeth called from her bedroom. "Who is that?"

Hearing where it came from made Mr. Darcy relieved. The sooner he could start his business, the sooner he could leave without being disturbed.

Turning to the servant, Julia, Mr. Darcy nodded to her.

"Stand sentinel in the corner while I am here," he instructed her, "for if you never leave, then I will have done nothing to harm Miss Bennet's reputation."

"Sir," Julia whispered, "you are already ruining it."

"No," he argued, "if her door remains closed, then I am only ruining mine."

Julia remained in the corner of the hallway.

"I shall never leave this spot," she warned.

"Julia?" Elizabeth called.

"Julia is here to be a chaperone for us," Mr. Darcy said through the door, "but Miss Bennet, it is Mr. Darcy. And I've come to speak with you."

CHAPTER 16

BLINDED BY HUBRIS

*W*hen hearing his voice, I was shocked and alarmed.

"Mr. Darcy," I gasped, rushing to the door and locking it. "Whatever are you doing in coming here?"

"I feel that it is necessary to speak with you on matters that we had discussed earlier."

"There is nothing more that we should speak about. We have talked enough already."

"Yes, we did speak, and then we walked away not knowing each other. Miss Bennet, we have grown to understand and accept each other's nature. We have embraced logic and rationality. We have discovered that we can become amiable with each other and hear the other speak their mind without anger or shame. And we have fallen away from that. I wish for us to return to that again if we are able. I only ask that you please hear me in what I say. I shall leave you afterward to form your opinions as you may. Miss Bennet, this is all that I ask."

When hearing him, I was in a torn state when it came to deciding where my desires truly fell. A part of me wished that he would leave and never speak to me again. But there was another side of me—which I could only assume was the side that was often tempted to press the papercut that one could sometimes get on one's finger—that was desirous to hear him.

Suddenly, I was hurled out of my indecision when I recalled

that I was in the bedroom of a house where I was the guest. And he —Mr. Darcy—was a man who was standing outside of my door. The impropriety of it was extreme, to say the least.

"Mr. Darcy," I rushed out, going to the other side of my door and making sure that it was locked, "you, more than anyone, know the dangers of our situation. I am a guest in a parsonage, and I am receiving a gentleman who is standing outside of my bedroom door. My reputation shall never recover from this."

"We are not alone, right, Miss Julia?"

"I am here," Julia said, "and Miss Bennet, I promise, I shall not leave this spot. Nor do I fully condone what is happening here. It is merely that…Mr. Darcy is so much stronger than myself, so I cannot move him. And if I leave to fetch help, then I shall leave you alone. Therefore, I am here."

"Thank you." I sighed, closing my eyes and resting against the doorway. "I suppose that I have no choice but to come out, and we may proceed to the sitting room. I just… I cannot face you now, sir."

"Then let us remain in this way. In truth, not seeing your face shall make it easier to divulge what I must. And going downstairs shall only waste the little time we have together anyway. First, I realize that some of the things I said perhaps hurt you. For that, I am sorry. And please, I beg of you to hear me speak, uninterrupted, so that I can tell you as much as I can."

"This is madness," Julia whispered under her breath.

"No, Miss Julia," Darcy retorted, "this is Kent."

This strange declaration distracted me, but I was not diverted, for the strangeness of the situation was still overpowering my calmness, and I could not arrive at anything else but perturbation. Truly, all of this was just too tiresome, and I felt as if I was in a whirlwind of confusion.

On the other side of the door, I heard Mr. Darcy clear his throat. Giving into the madness—for my curiosity had gotten the better of me—I sat down on the floor, leaning, facing the door. Under the crack in the doorway, I even saw Mr. Darcy's feet. Due to his nerves, I saw that sometimes he shifted in his place, trying to gather his courage.

"Mr. Darcy," I began, "I have agreed to listen to you. Begin, or I shall lose my patience with you."

"She is angry with me," I heard him say to Miss Julia.

"Anger is a pleasant way of phrasing what I feel," I augmented.

"Oh," Mr. Darcy sighed, and then he cleared his throat again. "First, pardon the freedom with which I demand your attention. Your feelings, I know, will bestow it unwillingly, but I demand it of your justice. Two offenses of a very different nature, you have laid down at my feet. The first mentioned was, that, regardless of the sentiments of either, I had detached Mr. Bingley from your sister. And the other, that I had, in defiance of various claims, in defiance of honor and humanity, ruined the immediate prosperity and blasted the prospects of Mr. Wickham. Willfully and wantonly to have thrown off the companion of my youth, the acknowledged favorite of my father, a young man who had scarcely any other dependence than on our patronage, and who had been brought up to expect its exertion, would be a depravity, that would be an offence. But from the severity of that blame, I shall endeavor to acquit myself of both those situations. Some of the things I say may overwhelm you and even disturb your happiness, but I desire for you to hear me out entirely before you fully turn away from everything that we have become to each other. I can only say I am sorry, again, for the pain you may experience from anything you may hear.

"First, I shall speak of my interference on behalf of your sister's potential future connection to my friend. I had not been long in Hertfordshire before I saw, in common with others, that Bingley preferred your elder sister to any other young woman in the country. But it was not until the evening of the dance at Netherfield that I had any apprehension of his feeling a serious attachment. I had often seen him in love before. At that ball, while I had the honor of dancing with you, I was first made acquainted, by Sir William Lucas's accidental information, that Bingley's attentions to your sister had given rise to a general expectation of their marriage. You heard it as well. Everyone expected your sister and Bingley to be married soon.

"From that moment, I observed my friend's behavior more

attentively, and I could then perceive that his partiality for Miss Bennet was beyond what I had ever witnessed in him. However, your sister was a different matter entirely. I watched her as well. Her look and manners were open, cheerful, and engaging as ever, but without any symptom of peculiar regard. And I remained convinced from the evening's scrutiny, that although she received his attentions with pleasure, she did not invite them by any participation of sentiment. Put simply, it seemed only as if she was flattered, but she was not *in* love with him. You and I are not fully strangers to the world, we've seen when others were not in love but were in love with *the idea* of being in love. If *you* have not been mistaken here, *I* must have been in error. Your superior knowledge of your sister must make the latter probable."

"It does, and I shall make no apology for it," I interrupted, unafraid to disturb his confession. "Sir, please believe me. My sister's serenity of nature is mixed with a desire to not impose upon the world by making her feelings too known. She worries of displaying her feelings too outward to the point of exposing herself to ridicule. Also...in her own way, she is somewhat bashful and does not always know how to display her feelings."

"But you must understand what that looks like to an outside observer," Mr. Darcy replied. "Concealing one's emotions is prudent, but is it always fruitful? Does it present immediate profit for the person? If a woman does not display her feelings, then how is any man to feel the encouragement, when no encouragement is presented? How can I see that she loved my friend when she never displayed it?"

When speaking this, I had to reflect. Once, Charlotte had warned me about Jane's serene and docile nature sometimes not offering up proper encouragement. And that showing less than she felt and not more was a detriment to obtaining a man's heart. But I felt it a foolish thing for Darcy to suppose. After all, how was he so very different than Jane?

As I remained silent, Darcy clearly felt that he was at liberty to continue.

"Yet," Darcy continued, "If it be so, if I have been misled by such error to inflict pain on her, your resentment has not been unreasonable. But I shall not scruple to assert that the serenity of your sister's countenance and air was such as might have given the most acute observer a conviction that, however amiable her temper, her heart was not likely to be easily touched. That I was desirous of believing her indifferent is certain—but I will venture to say that my investigation and decisions are not usually influenced by my hopes or fears. I did not believe her to be indifferent because I wished it, I believed it on impartial conviction, as truly as I wished it in reason."

Impartial conviction! I was enraged by his belief that he was doing any of this out of pure objectivity. He was a mind that was too much influenced by pride and prejudice to be truly objective on any subject.

"Even if you believe what you say," I added, "which I am dubious over, let us be frank. I know your nature, Mr. Darcy. And there are other factors which I know would make you find Jane undesirable for your friend. We are not a wealthy family, and there is a want of connection. These are natural obstacles that would offend a soul such as yours. Do not pretend like these were not deciding factors in your choosing."

"My objections to the marriage," he continued, "were also akin to those complaints that you have listed."

"But Mr. Bingley seemed to not care about that. So, what was it to you?"

"There were other causes of repugnance."

"What are they?"

"Perhaps I should not say."

"How, sir? If you hide what you feel, then how am I to know in what way we do not earn your good opinion?"

"It was a lack of refinement and a display of improper and crassness that I had witnessed. The situation of your mother's family, though objectionable, was *nothing* in comparison to that total want of propriety so frequently, so almost uniformly betrayed by herself, by your three younger sisters, and occasionally even by your father."

His words hung in the air around me, I felt their dampness fall over my shoulders and were a weight upon me. Every word of his stabbed me internally, and I felt my pride burst.

"Mr. Darcy," I sighed, pained, "that was the most hurtful thing you have said to me. And you have said quite a few things that have given me grief."

"Pardon me," he rushed out. "It pains me to offend you. But amidst your concern for the defects of your nearest relations, and your displeasure at this representation of them, let it give you consolation to consider that, you and your elder sister always conducted yourselves with the utmost dignity, decorum and honorable behavior. I will only say further that from what passed that evening, my opinion of all parties was confirmed, and every inducement heightened, which could have led me before to preserve my friend from what I esteemed a most unhappy connection. He left Netherfield for London, on the day following, as you, I am certain, remember, with the design of soon returning."

"And," I asked, "I take it that the part you played in this came next?"

"Yes, it did. The part which I acted is now to be explained. His sisters' uneasiness had been equally excited with my own. We spoke and debated about what we should do, and it was all settled. We shortly resolved on joining him directly in London. We accordingly went, and there I readily engaged in the office of pointing out to my friend the certain evils of such a choice. I gave every argument to him that I am giving you now. Very quickly, he believed that your sister did not fully care for him. He is modest, that is just his way. To convince him, therefore, that he had deceived himself, was no very difficult point. To persuade him against returning into Hertfordshire, when that conviction had been given, was scarcely the work of a moment. I cannot blame myself for having done thus much."

"You cannot?"

"No, because they were in the service of a friend who did not want to see one of his closest companions trapped in a loveless match with a family that would cause him distress."

I bit my lip once more. Despite myself, I hated to hear him speak.

"There is but one part of my conduct in the whole affair on which I do not reflect with satisfaction," he admitted.

"Really?" I asked, through gritted teeth. "And pray tell, what would that be?"

"It is that I condescended to adopt the measures of art so far as to conceal from him your sister's being in town."

"Ah, yes, you did know."

"Yes, I did."

"Like I said, you lied to me. I knew you were concealing truths from me, Mr. Darcy, but I gave you every opportunity to rectify that mistake. You never took the hero's way out."

"But I admit to my villainy now. I do not have to do it, but I do it of my own free will. Does that bring me no credit? Does that not soften my behavior? Yes, I did know that your sister was in London. So did Miss Bingley, despite that her brother was unaware of it. I did it because I worried that if Bingley saw your sister again, it might cause him pain or lead to him making a mistake and giving in to his heart's desire. Perhaps this concealment, this disguise was beneath me. It is done, however, and it was done with the best intentions. If I have wounded your sister's feelings, it was unknowingly done, and though the motives which governed me may to you very naturally appear insufficient, I have not yet learnt to condemn them."

"Then you still do not feel remorse for it," I summed up. "You feel that you have done right."

"I do."

I balled my right hand into a fist.

"Mr. Darcy, leave the parsonage now and give me peace. For, I can assure you that you have given me nothing else."

"Please, hear me out on the other point before you send me away."

"I want you to leave."

"I cannot until you hear my other complaint."

"If I listen, will you promise to leave me afterward?"

"Despite my desire to remain, yes, I will leave. If you wish it."

"I will, no matter what I feel. Then continue and be done with it."

"With respect to that other, more weighty accusation, of having injured Mr. Wickham, I can only refute it by laying before you the whole of his connection with my family. Of what he has *particularly* accused me, I am ignorant. Would you please tell me what he told you that I had done?"

"He told me that your father had left him an inheritance. Your father had left him a living at the church attached to your estate. He was to be a clergyman, but when your father died, and the living fell vacant, you refused, point blank, to honor your father's wishes. You gave the living to another man, and now Mr. Wickham is left to be reduced to a life of mild poverty."

"He lied!" Darcy hissed.

This bold and harsh declaration, in which Mr. Wickham's veracity was attacked, made me defensive, but also curious.

"You would say that," I responded, "but have you any proof? For I shall accept nothing else less than solid evidence to dissuade me that Mr. Wickham ever expressed a falsehood a day in his life."

"I can assure you, Miss Bennet, that since reaching his manhood, he has never told a truth for one full day."

"This is a serious accusation."

"Is it any graver than the accusations that he had laid at my door?"

"Once more, I ask for proof."

"And I shall give it. Not only will I tell you the truth, but I can summon more than one witness of undoubted veracity. Everything that I tell you now you can ask of my cousin, Colonel Fitzwilliam. He will support everything I say and recount it in the precise way that I tell it."

He mentioned Colonel Fitzwilliam, who was a man who, since meeting him, showed me nothing else but an open nature. If the Colonel could be brought to validate an account, then perhaps I would reconsider where my sympathies lay.

"Mr. Wickham is the son of a very respectable man. My father respected him. And George Wickham was his godson. My father supported him at school, and afterward at Cambridge—most important assistance, as his own father, always poor from the extravagance of his wife, would have been unable to give him a gentleman's education. My father was not only fond of this young man's society, but he had also the highest opinion of him, and hoping the church would be his profession, intended to provide for him in it. You know Mr. Wickham. He is a charming man, and his manner is always engaging.

As I said to you before, he always shall have a talent at making friends, but he cannot ever keep them. When going to school together, I saw the true man that Wickham was. The vicious propensities—the want of principle, which he was careful to guard from the knowledge of our fathers, could not escape the observation of a young man of nearly the same age with himself, and who had opportunities of seeing him in unguarded moments. Here again, I shall give you pain—to what degree you only can tell. Mr. Wickham was wanton, promiscuous with his attentions to women, took many a woman's virtue, and cared not for how he left. He also rang up debts, that out of my honor, I discharged for him. He was lax in his studies, he gambled frequently, and cared only for the pleasures that he could receive from life, without any of the work and labor that goes to building the reputation of a respectable man."

When hearing this narration, I shut my eyes. Mr. Wickham was not such a man. No, he was not!

"He also would prove to be a fortune hunter," Darcy continued. "And I shall relate to you the woman whose life he almost ruined with his greed. My excellent father died about five years ago, and his attachment to Mr. Wickham was to the last so steady, that in his will he particularly recommended it to me to give Wickham the living of the church at Pemberly—and if he took orders, desired that a valuable family living might be his as soon as it became vacant. There was also a legacy of one thousand pounds. His own father did not long survive mine, and within half a year from these events, Mr. Wickham wrote to inform me that, having finally resolved against taking orders, he hoped I should not think it unreasonable for him to expect some more immediate pecuniary advantage, in lieu of the preferment, by which he could not be benefited. He had some intention, he added, of studying law, and I must be aware that the interest of one thousand pounds would be a very insufficient support therein. I rather wished than believed him to be sincere. But, at any rate, was perfectly ready to accede to his proposal. I knew that Mr. Wickham ought not to be a clergyman. The business was therefore soon settled—he resigned all claim to assistance in the church, were it possible that he could ever be in a situation to receive it and accepted in return three thousand pounds. There, Miss Bennet. I did not deny him the living, but rather, he chose not to inherit and was given money instead. Money that, I know, he gambled away within months of our ceasing our acquaintance."

He paused at this moment, and I suppose he was waiting for me to speak, but I could find no reply to return. I was too stunned.

"All connection between us seemed now dissolved," Darcy continued. "I thought too ill of him to invite him to Pemberley or admit his society in town. In town I believe he chiefly lived, but his studying the law was a mere pretense, and now being free from all restraint, his life was a life of idleness and dissipation. For about three years, I heard little of him. Yet on the decease of the incumbent of the living which had been designed for him, he applied to me again by letter for the presentation. His circumstances, he assured me, and I had no difficulty in believing it, were exceedingly bad. He had found the law a most unprofitable study, and was now absolutely resolved on being ordained, if I would present him to the living in question—of which he trusted there could be little doubt, as he was well assured that I had no other person to provide for, and I could not have forgotten my revered father's intentions. You will hardly blame me for refusing to comply with this entreaty, or for resisting every repetition to it. I knew that this enraged him, but I did not care—and he was doubtless as violent in his abuse of me to others. He always looks for someone to pity him. But this wasn't the end, for he would soon find other ways of getting his revenge on me. For last summer, he stumbled upon a young woman who was wealthy, and who I was connected with. She was but fifteen years old.

About a year ago, this young woman was taken from school,

and an establishment formed for her in London. Last summer she went with the lady named Mrs. Younge, who presided over it, to Ramsgate, and thither also went Mr. Wickham, undoubtedly by design. To my surprise, Mrs. Younge and Mr. Wickham were very good friends. Therefore, we were all deceived in her character. When arriving, Mr. Wickham offered his attention to the young lady of wealth, this fifteen-year-old girl, whose affectionate heart retained a strong impression of his kindness to her as a child, that she was persuaded to believe herself in love, and to consent to an elopement.

Mr. Wickham intentionally sought a young woman out, seduced her, and was going to marry her for her wealth…for the thirty thousand pounds she had inherited. The only reason that young woman was saved, was because I went to visit her. I joined them unexpectedly a day or two before the intended elopement, and the young lady, unable to support the idea of grieving me, whom she almost looked up to as a father, acknowledged the whole to me. You may imagine what I felt and how I acted. I wrote to Mr. Wickham, who left the place immediately, and Mrs. Younge was, of course, removed from her charge. Mr. Wickham's chief object was unquestionably this young lady's fortune. Yet I cannot help supposing that the hope of revenging himself on me was a strong inducement. His revenge would have been complete indeed."

When hearing the end of this, I was dubious, to say the least. This was not in Wickham's style.

"Mr. Darcy," I began. "I cannot believe this of him."

"Mr. Wickham will always possess the appearance of being a veracious man, but he shall never have the credit of it. You must believe me in this."

"You have given accusations, but still there is no proof. I suppose you do not divulge the young lady's name for fear of exposing her."

"She was young. Therefore, I feel that her age has the right to excuse her."

"Too right, it would. However, how am I to believe you when, for all that I know, this is vicious defamation and slander? This young woman may very well not even exist."

"She does exist."

"But I would be a fool to believe it without any sort of proof. You say that Colonel Fitzwilliam knows as well, but if I were to attack him on such a subject, I would not even know where to begin."

"If I were to offer the identity of the woman who I speak of, would you swear yourself to secrecy? Please, promise me that you will not tell another soul."

"We are at a strange place of stalemate. Yes, I would keep her secret, but I have no right to know her name."

"If it will help you to learn what Wickham really is, then I have no choice but to confess it. But again, promise me that you shall never reveal this to anyone?"

I felt like a horror for ever considering knowing the name of a woman whose secret had every right to remain with her. However, if I were to believe Darcy, then a woman without a name would prove to be a useless thing and make me appear as easy to persuade.

"Very well," I allowed, "I promise, I shall never tell another living soul."

"Do you have a pen and paper in your room? If you do, can you slip it under the door, and I shall write the name? Once you are done reading it, I implore you to throw the name into the fire so any evidence of it shall fade away forever."

"All of that, I can do." I went to my desk, pulled out the pen, paper, and slid them both under the doorway. As I did so, Mr. Darcy's and my fingertips touched slightly before we pulled them away.

I waited for him to finish writing. Once, he had to give the pen back to me so that I could re-dip the tip in ink. Soon the paper returned to me. Snatching it up quickly, I unfolded the paper, and a few words were written.

My sister, Miss Georgiana Darcy

When seeing the words, they rang out in my mind, and I was silenced.

It couldn't be!

Mr. Wickham had tried to elope with Miss Georgiana Darcy, Mr. Darcy's little sister, who was only fifteen years old? My mind was overcome. One moment I was doubting it, another moment, I was considering the veracity of it.

"You swear to this!" I gasped through the door.

"Yes, I do."

There was a slight pause.

"I am not a villain, Miss Bennet. I simply am a friend who made the best decisions that he thought were right at the time, and an older person who had to protect someone that he swore to protect."

We were interrupted by Miss Julia.

"Mr. Darcy," she urged, "you must quit the house now, sir. I see Mrs. Collins and her family walking up the side path."

"Thank you," he rushed out, but I was too frozen to say anything. "Miss Bennet, I must leave you now."

"Yes," I whispered, "yes, I suppose that you must."

I heard him pay Miss Julia some coins and requested that she keep this all a secret—something that I would see to it that she did for as long as I could, and he rushed downstairs, where Miss Julia showed him out.

From my window, I saw him meet Charlotte, Sir William, and Maria on the walk, and then he begged their pardon and went back to Rosings.

And I remained sitting on the floor, lost in all the confusion that lay at my feet.

CHAPTER 17

THE OVERPOWERING TRUTH

*W*hen Charlotte had returned, she immediately inquired about if I had seen Mr. Darcy. I opened my mouth, closed it, and then thought that a lie was perfectly appropriate for the circumstances. I told her that I spoke to him for merely a few minutes and that he had dashed off soon after his arrival. The moment was provocative. For after being told something so very disorientating requires a half day's reflection at least, where one sits down in quiet contemplation.

Unfortunately, I was not given any such time. I was immediately forced to be civil, appear unoccupied, and be casual in my manner.

"No wonder that Mr. Darcy's stay was brief," Maria had informed me as she removed her coat and bonnet, "since he shall be leaving tomorrow morning."

"He is leaving?" I asked, surprised at this news.

"Well, yes."

"He only came for the purpose of assisting his aunt in choosing a new parson for Hunsford," Charlotte voiced, "and Lady Catherine informed us that her pursuits had been achieved. I shall commit to leaving Hunsford Parsonage in a week's time, and then a new reverend will take residence here, I shall return to Lucas Lodge and then we shall be as we once were."

I could tell that she looked downcast when she said this.

"I do not believe that there will ever be such a thing as being what one once was," I countered. Charlotte looked at me strangely, but I felt it best to redirect my attitude; therefore, I attempted to look livelier.

"Well," I continued, "if Darcy is to leave tomorrow, will Colonel Fitzwilliam take his leave with him?"

"Yes, I do believe that both men are determined to travel at the same time," Sir William reported, "which makes me quite sad. For I would have liked them to remain here while we did so. Their departure will make our dinners quite sad and less cheery."

"Then, we shall have to bear the deprivation of their company with spirit," I countered, to hide my nerves. "And let us see if Lady Catherine can even bear our company when they are gone. I do believe that compared to them, she may think very little of us."

"I do not think it shall be precisely so," Charlotte observed. "I get the sense that she will miss us being present. For, when we depart, she will have no one to order around."

"Yes, for to her, we are all chess pieces."

We all sat down together, but I desperately desired to be alone at the time.

Maria and Sir William both gave me detailed accounts of what happened at the dinner and I but half listened. My mind was still dwelling on the small paper that Mr. Darcy had given me, revealing that Mr. Wickham had attempted to elope with his little sister.

Fortunately, Sir William and Maria were fatigued and wished to retire early. This contented me, and as we were all separating to go to our different parts of the home, I crossed paths with Miss Julia.

In a very casual manner, I took her arm.

"Miss Julia," I whispered, "forgive me, but I must ask. Were you given remuneration for your silence on what happened earlier?"

"Yes, ma'am," she whispered back. "Four whole pounds of remuneration."

"That is a proper sum." Then I gave her one more pound. "I beg of you, let it help you keep to your silence, even long after the gentleman is gone."

She looked at me squarely in the face.

"What gentleman do you speak of? For I know of no man who ever addressed me in the way that you speak."

I smiled and released her. She was an obliging woman. She was already set to forget the entire situation already.

Oh, sometimes money solved things greatly!

Before we fully retired for bed, I went to Charlotte's room. Knocking on her door, she opened it and ushered me inside.

"Us sitting together like this," Charlotte said, "it reminds me of the times when often you would spend the night at Lucas Lodge."

"Then let us talk freely as we used to," I encouraged, "for we often could tell secrets to each other there."

"You wish to tell secrets now."

"Charlotte, you are determined to be happy and to return to our lives at Lucas Lodge. And I can see that. Do you stress this happiness to try and encourage yourself to forget about your present state of things? Forgive me for asking, but I merely wished to know, for perhaps you wished to speak more on the matter, but you were afraid of how to approach the subject."

Charlotte looked down at her hands.

"You were correct earlier," she admitted, "that try as one might, one cannot ever fully go back. I am happy to return to Lucas Lodge because that is home. However, I also do not want to return, Lizzy. I dread the looks of pity from the people in Meryton, but also to see my old home, knowing that I shall return to it in the same way as I left it… I do not want to face that. Try as one might, we cannot go back."

"But you must. And people will pity you, for a while. Fortunately, you shall recover, and there is nothing wrong with Longbourn being Longbourn, and Lucas Lodge being as it always was to you—home. You can start again, just in a different direction."

"I liked being able to run my own home. I did not love Mr. Collins, but I did love the independence that I received in the bargain. Besides, he did not love me either. He only married me out of spite. Therefore, I need not feel wicked for what I say."

"I will not judge you."

"Thank you. You are one of the few people that I know who has the right to judge me. Therefore, I am grateful that you refrain from doing so."

"Yes, though I am sorely tempted," I teased. "However, I should know so that I am prepared. Tomorrow, do you think Mr. Darcy and the Colonel shall come to take their leave?"

"I suspect they shall. It is the proper thing. Why do you ask?"

"No particular reason."

Charlotte gave me a look.

"What?" I asked.

"Is there a particular Colonel you wish to see before he leaves?" she asked pointedly.

"Charlotte, you are mistaken." I grinned and added, "I am not in any danger. The Colonel has made it very evident that he must marry a woman of wealth, and I am not wealthy. In fact, my feelings for him have always been nothing more than cordial. It is simply that it would look improper of me to not be here when they leave, so I must be certain not to take my morning walk until the middle of the day."

"Ah, propriety."

I bit my lip and then thought that I ought to consider something. Gathering my courage, I began to inquire.

"Charlotte, do you recall a conversation that we had before, about Jane. When we first noticed Bingley's taking an interest in her. Recall that while his partiality was clear, Jane's was not as present."

"Yes. And I remain firm in my assessment."

"You do?"

"Yes. We are all fools when it comes to love. Bingley liked Jane, enormously. But consider, he did not know her character. I believed that by not displaying her feelings for him in a more outward manner, she did not help him on. When it comes to love, there must be a certain vanity about us. We need to feel that our love is being returned in the same mode, manner and matter in which we are expressing it ourselves. And forgive me for speaking so, Lizzy, but I cannot help but priding myself in being correct in this case. For look? Despite my present circumstances, Mr. Collins *did* propose to me. Yes, it was because he was using me as a distraction from his wounded pride from you rejecting him. But he still did make me an offer. And he made it because I displayed all the outward things which you display when you are trying to attract a man. I did not have Jane's beauty. However, all that beauty in the world will not alter the fact that she did not display the symptoms of a woman in love. If she had, then I doubt that Mr. Bingley would have been able to leave her and then forget her just because he changed locations."

"So," I furthered, "say that you were a man, and you had met Jane. You were enchanted by her beauty, her sweetness and her serenity of nature. But you do not think that you would have continued pursuing her because she did not act like a woman in love? Because she never expressed it?"

"Precisely. A pretty face can only take you so far. Besides, the world is filled with pretty faces and serene natures. Soon after the novelty of that beauty wears off, what can hold a man's attention to you if you never made him feel…special to you? And to show you the littleness of how she presented herself, I felt that you and Darcy displayed more direct attention to each other than ever Jane did to Bingley."

I was silent over this. At first, when Mr. Darcy had spoken of Jane's appearance of being indifferent to Bingley, I thought his observations were too preposterous. But now, time can often be one's best friend and offer the best council. For, as Charlotte had said, Bingley *did not* know Jane's character, as I had. Nor did Darcy for that matter. Therefore, who was I to expect Darcy or anyone to immediately understand Jane's character when they were never familiar with it from the start? I had been blinded by prejudice towards and against the wrong impressions of things. Therefore, how could I expect Bingley to feel the sort of romantic emotions that Jane never showed? I felt miserable at that moment, and truly humbled.

"I wish I had listened to you from the start," I informed Charlotte, "for, as much as it hurts my pride to admit, you were correct."

"Thank you," Charlotte responded, "and know that I said those things out of a desire to help your family, and not to criticize it."

"I know. I just wish I had come to see the sense of it sooner. I could have warned Jane. I could have advised her."

"Is Mr. Bingley engaged to another woman?"

"I have not heard that he is."

"Then why is it too late? Why can you not tell her, and see if something will come of it?"

I looked squarely at her.

"So, you do not think that I should give up either?"

"Were you going to give up, to begin with?"

"No, I was not."

"No, I could tell that you were not. So, follow your instincts. Fight."

"You still really are my friend."

"I never stopped being it. I just had no choice but to make the best decision for myself."

I kissed her on the cheek and went to my room.

All night, I had a hard time sleeping. Though, fortunately, I was soon not to remain in anxiety. The next morning, I would see Mr. Darcy and the Colonel again. I could appeal to the Colonel to verify the veracity of Mr. Darcy's tale…though I was slowly beginning to accept the reality that Mr. Darcy was correct.

For indeed, the more that I thought on it all, the more I began to see the many moments of impropriety on Mr. Wickham's side.

He had been the one to randomly begin the subject of my acquaintance with Mr. Darcy.

He had been the one to offer his tale of Mr. Darcy's cheating him of his inheritance in a manner where I did not have a long enough acquaintance for him to entrust me with such a tale of his history.

He also said that he would courageously face Mr. Darcy always. Yet, he lied! At the Netherfield ball, Mr. Darcy had remained, but Mr. Wickham was the one who fled the county until the event was at an end.

He was the one who had informed me that he would tell no

living soul, besides me, about how Mr. Darcy had robbed him of his due, but when Mr. Darcy left Hertfordshire, he began to tell everyone of it.

And the way in which he described Mr. Darcy cheating him out of the inheritance was also laughable and foolish. I had been so very blind, allowing my prejudice to ignore all these obvious signs of dishonesty, hypocrisy and crass behavior. I was feeling a little humbled.

Even now, Wickham's dissolving the attachment to Miss King felt like I had heard the wrong side of things. I wondered if maybe Kitty had been told a false rumor and that Miss King's uncle had been the one to break off the engagement between them, seeing that Wickham was a fortune hunter.

When Colonel Fitzwilliam arrived, that was when I knew that I would be fully satisfied of what to feel. And then, I would know how to act.

Whatever the truth was, there was one thing I knew I would do; I would make peace with Mr. Darcy. Even if it meant that I had to single him out and seek out his company before he left, I was going to attempt to reach a delicate amicability with him.

For indeed, I had nothing to gain by keeping him as my enemy.

The next day, we were all assembled in the sitting room, awaiting the two men to come and pay their respects to take their leave. I was so very anxious to see them both. Admittedly, I wished to see Mr. Darcy in particular.

Therefore, my shock was immense, and my disappointment even larger when we did receive a visit—and it was merely just the Colonel himself.

He said all the correct things to say when you are departing from a county, and they were all casually voiced…truly, the Colonel would always be so very gifted with how he presented himself. In that moment, I would have been ever so happy to know that there was at least one man in the world who had both all the goodness, but also all the appearance of it as well.

While he did speak plainly and perfectly, I desired to have a private interview with him.

Despite that it would look too forward, once he sat down near me, and there was no one else to hear, I leaned in and whispered to him:

"Colonel, forgive me, but there is some information and advice that I require from you. I apologize for being so forward, but I wish to make these inquiries in private. Can you please request to take a stroll about the gardens so that we can speak?"

Despite that this was an inappropriate thing to ask, the Colonel did not take it amiss nor rebuke me. Rather, he turned to Charlotte and asked if he could take a stroll about the greenery, for one last time.

Charlotte accepted this. I offered my services to join him, he readily accepted, we got our things on, and we walked outside.

"Well," the Colonel began, "you have resorted to secrecy to get my attention."

"I did, and while I feel obliged to you for not forsaking me, my brash side does not apologize."

"Well, you have my attention, and I am curious to see what you do with it."

"Yesterday, your cousin came to see me, and I might have accused him of behavior that he was innocent of. He gave me an account of himself and then said that I could appeal to you to verify his statements. I am going to ask you about something, and again, recall that he told me that I could come to you to help convince me of what the truth is."

"Your tone is serious."

"Because he told me a secret that was serious. He told me a story about a man named Mr. Wickham, and the crime he may have committed to your cousin and your charge, Miss Georgiana Darcy."

At the mention of this, Colonel Fitzwilliam's face fell, and his eyes darkened.

"I see that I have your attention in full," I stated.

I told the Colonel everything that had occurred between myself and Mr. Darcy the day before. I also told him about what Mr. Wickham had told me when we first met.

When I finished narrating everything, Colonel Fitzwilliam was enraged, to say the least.

"That libertine!" he hissed. "That absolute rake and ruffian. For truly, does Wickham have any honor in him? If he did, then he lost it long ago."

I blinked at this declaration.

"So," I gathered, "Mr. Darcy was telling me the truth? He never cheated Wickham out of his inheritance at all, and he did try to elope with Miss Darcy?"

"Yes," the Colonel said, "all of that was true. Mr. Wickham has injured everyone who he owed so very much to. He treated Darcy and Georgiana in an infamous manner, and I swear, Miss Bennet, he is the worst of men."

I bit my lip and looked ahead as we walked.

"Then I have been a fool," I declared.

"It is not your fault," Colonel Fitzwilliam said. "Wickham was born with many natural charms to him, and for them to be compiled with the other charms that he has learned in life, it has made him the sort that is easy to fall prey to. We all fall victim to those sorts at one time or another. The trick is not about never encountering them, no, or even to see the truth behind them, to begin with. Those sorts will *always* trick us, at first. For individuals like that, the trick is simply to realize that they tricked you and avoid it ever happening again in the future. We all are the fool at some point in our lives."

"And there will always be that person who triumphs over us."

"Sadly, yes."

"You speak from experience on this. So, you know how I feel."

"Yes, I do. Why do you think I have chosen to always be so very pleasant? Individuals like myself choose to be this way because we suffered at the hands of those who were not."

"Poor Colonel."

"Yes, well, perhaps I ought not to complain. Others have it worse than me. Also, if it helps you, then believe that there was a time

NEY MITCH

when I believed Wickham to be a good man as well. Then I learned the truth. Miss Bennet, he is one of the worst men I have ever met. He cares nothing for the feelings of others, but only appeals to them out of vanity. His interest is not in loving others. His interest is that he needs to be loved. I want to believe he shall improve his mind one day, but nothing is ever fully certain. All that he said against Darcy were lies, I can assure you, and vicious slander."

"I believed the wrong man…and I can see, from your coming alone, that Mr. Darcy has left already."

"He left this morning and would not wait to set out with me. I was hurt at his not traveling with me, for we usually come and depart from Rosings together, but I could tell that he needed time to be alone."

"And the need to avoid seeing me for as long as he possibly could. I am not afraid of deducing this, Colonel. I suppose it is what I deserve. Thank you for enlightening me on everything."

"And I have your word that you shall not reveal these secrets to another?"

"I shall not," I vowed. "Except that this does present some awkwardness."

"How so?"

"Well, Wickham is such a man that he is not to be trusted. I will say nothing, but by doing so, I do not warn people about his true nature."

"Oh, I had not thought of that. Well, that is not sound nor correct. He clearly has not attempted to establish his character correctly. Still, I do not want Georgiana's reputation to ever be risked. If Wickham appears as being dangerous, warn people that he is not to be trusted, that you have received information that shows his tales of being mistreated are false but give no particulars on the subject. If you want to rectify your claims against my cousin, then you have the right to clear his name of any such crime that Wickham has laid down to it."

"That is very wise. It will be hard, for despising Mr. Darcy is something that people love to do in Hertfordshire. In my attempting to claim his innocence, I might send some of them into an apoplectic fit, because I will overturn all that they believe," I jested lightly, "but yes, it must be attempted."

"And, when I write to Darcy again, I will inform him of our conversation. It would do well for you both to know that the other now understands each other."

"Thank you," I responded. "I doubt that we shall meet again, but I cannot bear the idea of us moving about in the world and willfully misunderstanding each other. I have had enough of that for a lifetime."

"It was a pleasure to have met you, Miss Bennet."

"And I with you. And after this, where do you and Darcy go? Will you see him again very soon? Or will the war take you away from England soon after you leave the serenity of the country?"

"Well, first, I shall join Darcy at his townhouse, which he will remain at for a month complete. Afterward, we have been invited to Canter's Abbey. It's the seat of Sir Aleck Granger. He's a friend of our family's. I shall be happy for a brief while. After then, duty calls me to mind my station, and I am to be shipped off to the peninsula."

This news was precisely what I wished to hear!

"Then steal happiness while you can, Colonel. We do not often get it as much as we wish we had."

Eventually, Colonel Fitzwilliam took his leave of us, and I knew that I would miss him.

There were very few men in the world who were such as him.

CHAPTER 18

CHARLOTTE LUCAS; THE WOMAN WHO IS FULL OF SURPRISES

*C*olonel Fitzwilliam and Mr. Darcy were gone. And thus, ended part of my expectations and many of my anxieties.

Fortunately, never to remain out of spirits for long, I gathered my resolve. Dwelling on the past would never change anything. Self-pity is a contagious thing, and often one chooses to remain in it because it gives the mind something to dwell upon. Yet, I have often regarded that state of mind as an addictive one; you enjoy feeling melancholic rather than rise out of it and look for a solution.

I refused to do that ever, and therefore I refused to do that now. But rather, I was now going to look toward a stronger horizon and find another step to help all be put to rights.

After all, we still were not certain that Longbourn was ours.

But what I was certain about was that Bingley loved Jane, and Jane loved Mr. Bingley. Therefore, *getting them to reunite* was still my chief cause. For if Jane gained a husband who could provide for all of us, then I had secured our future. I felt terrible that we would impose on Mr. Bingley so very much, for in that moment I imagined my mother being at Netherfield Park. God, my mother! She would drive Mr. Bingley to distraction!

Although if I were to be there, then I could assist in moderating her behavior and attempt to do my best to remove her from Bingley's society for as long as I could. That would lead to me being always in my mother's company, but Jane's happiness was worth my hell.

Therefore, no, I was *not* to remain in cold prudence, sit still, and do nothing. If I lost the game, it would not be from not striving for it!

I had another plan. After leaving Hunsford, we were going to break our journey in London, where I would see Jane.

But Mr. Darcy was still in London. And he would be there when I would visit Cheapside.

What I had in mind was presumptuous, and I would risk much. Still! Fortune often did favor the bold.

Now that the two men were gone, Rosings Park did, in fact, feel their loss. Therefore, when going to the park to visit Lady Catherine, we found ourselves as guests that the great lady welcomed tremendously.

"My we shall be easily forlorn now that Darcy and the dear Colonel have left us," she announced. "They are such very delightful men and so ever attached to me. They always miss Rosings Park when they leave it."

"I find," Charlotte said, "that all must regret leaving this place when their time has come."

"You sound even more somber than they, Mrs. Collins."

"Well, yes," Charlotte admitted, "if you must know. I have grown very fond of these woods and hills, and you and my husband had done everything to make Hunsford Parsonage comfortable for me. Indeed, I have spent some of the happiest times of my life here in Kent. Do you not agree, father and Maria?"

"Yes," Sir William stuttered. "I declare that I have never been more amazed and awestruck with such grandeur and elegance until I came here. This home, and Kent itself, displays the very essence of what made my time at St. James's Court so very memorable for me."

"Well," Lady Catherine said, turning to me, "you do not speak up, Miss Bennet. You have barely spoken two words since you came here. Are you out of spirits yourself?"

"No, indeed, madam," I stated.

"Yes, you are, for you shall be going yourself. But since your mother is recently widowed, I shall not implore you to remain here, though you ought to. You all should remain, for surely, you have nothing else to do that is as important as remaining. No one ever does."

"For," Charlotte continued, "Rosings Park commands an important place within us all."

Charlotte's compliment here suited the lady perfectly fine, but for some reason, it made me alert. For Charlotte's compliments savored strongly of obsequiousness. In fact, her tone reminded me of… Mr. Collins himself.

Lady Catherine then returned to her favorite discussion: her nephews.

"Do you know?" she began, "that Darcy and the Colonel visit me more often than my other relations? And they are always sad to leave me. Their attachment to Rosings Park always increases, yet with Darcy, his attachment is clearly the closest. For when he departed this morning, his expression was heavy, and I marveled at it. I do declare that soon, he shall wish to always remain at Rosings Park," and here she looked at Anne de Bourgh, "and a certain desirable event will take place."

I looked between Anne and her mother. Once more, Anne de Bourgh showed no signs of partiality toward the mention of Darcy's name.

Still, Lady Catherine was determined to have him for a son-in-law, despite that they both obviously felt nothing for each other. How often marriage has nothing to do with the people involved, but rather, is between third parties who all are acting out of blind prejudice and preference.

Anne did not love Darcy.

Darcy clearly did not love Anne.

And Lady Catherine clearly did not care one way or the other about this sad truth.

I knew how this was all to end.

Mr. Darcy and Anne would never be married, and that was how it was all going to be.

"Well," Charlotte said, "on that joyful day, you shall be very happy, Lady Catherine."

"I believe that I shall."

"Yes," Maria echoed, "very happy."

"It is a strange sort of sensation, though," Lady Catherine voiced. "For we mothers always strive so very hard for our daughters to make a success of themselves. And, therein lies the irony of it. We are happy to part with them, but also saddened that we must part with them. We aim all our lives for our children to marry well, and then when they do, they leave us."

"But Anne shall never leave," Charlotte supported, "for when she marries, the man will remain here at Rosings Park, and you will not have lost a daughter, but gained a son."

"Well, yes," Lady Catherine smirked, "now that is a happy thought indeed, for I had not considered it for the moment. Mrs. Collins, I never noticed that you were of such a supportive nature. For, I had much influence on your late husband, as you know, and I always said that he ought to marry. I said, chose wisely and carefully. I said that she also ought to be an active and useful sort of person—not brought up too highly. Sir William, though you are of elevated rank, you still made certain that your daughters were brought up in the proper manner. Therefore, though they are not, and could never be, of Anne's rank, you did right by them."

"Lady Catherine," Sir William gasped, "I thank you! Truly, this is so much praise!"

Maria giggled, her cheeks reddened, and then she was silent.

The rest of the day was spent in this manner, where Charlotte was doing everything in her power to bestow her abilities at pleasing.

However, it was merely an observation. I did not concern myself with it, for it gave me time to not be talkative and make plans for the immediate future. I merely assumed that Charlotte's eagerness to compliment and flatter Lady Catherine was because she desired to leave a good impression before she was to leave Kent forever.

Her behavior was a little too verbose and flattering for my taste, but I did not care one way or the other about it.

Whenever Anne de Bourgh was to stand up, Charlotte complimented her gown or how she looked. She asked if Anne wished to partake in cards or backgammon, in order to give Mrs. Jenkinson time away from tending to her charge.

Charlotte also asked Lady Catherine if she needed a pillow to be placed behind her back for support. Every now and again, Maria echoed Charlotte's words or actions, and Sir William smiled, proud of Charlotte.

When we sat down to dinner, Charlotte complimented the food and the dishes. She also began to eagerly inquire about Anne and if she desired to travel to many places.

This was more attention than I had ever seen Charlotte give Anne before.

Our visit passed eventually, and we returned home, only to return to Rosings every day, up until our departure. And each day, Charlotte found herself always being at Anne de Bourgh's disposal or appealing to Lady Catherine's vanity. She was often complimenting everything. And it was not until the last day of our meeting at the fancy home that I understood Charlotte's motive for being so obsequious and overtly charming.

"Sir William," Lady Catherine stated, "I have come to a decision that I believe that you shall find suitable."

"Yes, pray tell what it is?" Sir William gasped, always amazed at when she spoke with him.

"I have decided that Mrs. Collins is not to leave Kent."

"But I fear that I must, madam," Charlotte said, "for the new reverend is to take over."

"You will not be staying at the parsonage," Lady Catherine corrected, "but rather, I have a desire for you to remain here at Rosings Park, as another companion for Anne."

This news made my eyes widen, and Sir William and Maria gasped. Before I would allow my own reaction, I considered Charlotte's. She smiled, but surprise never reached her eyes. And I knew what was finally occurring; she was expecting to be invited because she had been planning this the whole time!

"Now that is generosity itself!" Sir William declared. "Lady Catherine, I am beside myself. I cannot thank you enough."

"Truly, I cannot as well, madam," Charlotte added, "and I am overjoyed and would love to remain at Rosings Park. Anne, I promise to serve you well and be a delightful companion to you."

Anne smiled at this but said nothing else.

"And," Lady Catherine added, "if Charlotte proves to be a valuable companion, then I would offer her sister, Maria, to come and visit often as well, and Miss Bennet, since all of your sisters are *out*, then I find that meeting them would not be something I would find disagreeable."

Maria was so shocked at this kind offer that her mouth dropped open. I smiled, and my response was serene, to say the least.

Sir William spoke enough for us both, while I offered all the proper kind words that one ought to give at the time. In truth, however, while I did have fond memories of Rosings Park, I was not certain if I desired to return there again. And Lady Catherine's inviting me was never out of a desire for my true companionship, but rather because she liked having company about her. She was an actress without a stage, but she had a drawing room, and therefore, all she needed to supply it was an audience.

But Charlotte!

It now all made sense.

"Charlotte?" I questioned, "why?"

It had been an hour since we returned to Hunsford Parsonage, and Charlotte's things were packed, but now we were no longer taking them back to Lucas Lodge. Rather, Lady Catherine would send servants to the parsonage the next afternoon to have Charlotte's things brought up to Rosings.

Now, we were sitting in her bedroom as she was undoing her hair.

"Lizzy," Charlotte began, "what do you mean by asking me that? Lady Catherine asked me to stay on and become a companion for her daughter, and I have every right to agree to it. It is a very eligible position."

"And it is something that you did everything to obtain, by the use of flattery and charm," I pointed out, "this offer was not a surprise to you, for you were aiming for it. Charlotte, do not deny it, for you are not entirely innocent and without motive."

"If you were correct, then what would I be guilty of?"

"So, you admit that you had a plan through this all. You walked into Lady Catherine's sitting room this entire week, with an express desire to appeal to Lady Catherine's vanity, so that she would make you an offer."

"I do not deny it, Lizzy. And I never shall."

"But as I asked before, why? Why would you do that? You were almost able to finally go home. It was your desire for everything to be as it once was."

"Until you said something that I had to acknowledge was correct; we cannot ever fully go back. Try as we might."

"You could have tried, though. You are not like me; you have a home where your brothers will inherit it, and therefore no one shall ever throw you out on the street."

"No one was ever going to throw you all from out of Longbourn," Charlotte swore, "you know that I was never going to let that happen. But Lizzy, even if I could go back to the life I had, would I want to? I would return to being a burden on my parents. I would go back to being a woman with no prospects. And then it occurred to me, I did not want to return to that state. I did not want to be an object of pity! I wanted to be independent. And this way, I can be. Also, in this way, I cost my family no money, and perhaps even make money in turn. This, perhaps, is the best option for me. I shall miss you, but I have to look to the future."

Seeing the sense of her thoughts, I laid down on her bed and looked up at the ceiling. It was a blank white color. For some reason, the blankness of it all antagonized me.

"And," Charlotte continued, "by the way that you sound, you speak as if I have committed a crime by looking for solutions to my predicament. You observe my actions with an unfriendly eye. I would not have thought you, Lizzy, of all people, would find offense in me taking control of my life, and becoming a woman of action, rather than inaction."

"No," I stated, still looking up at the ceiling, "I do not blame you for your actions, or judge you. I just wanted to make certain that you knew what you were about, and that you were doing things for reasons that would prove to not be harmful to yourself or anyone around you. I will never cast aspersions at a friend for going to life rather than waiting for life to happen to her."

"Precisely. Some of us cannot wait for adventure to come to us. Sometimes, we have to go to it. I am that sort of woman, Lizzy."

"Yes. You are. I suppose that I was only disconcerted for a moment because I saw something else in you that frightened me."

"And what was that?" Charlotte asked. "Go on and admit it. I am not afraid of you."

"I could not help but wonder. The way that you recommended yourself to Lady Catherine, was that the same way that you endeared yourself to Mr. Collins?"

The question hung about the air for a moment.

"Charlotte," I pressed, "the way that you had Lady Catherine become attached to you, was that the same system and habit that you used to get Mr. Collins to fall in love with you?"

"We both know that he was never in love with me."

"Very well, then I shall rephrase. Did you use that system to convince Mr. Collins to get him to think that he was in love with you?"

"Yes, I did. Those were both the same method. I can see that you are unsettled by it."

"I am just afraid that there is a side of you that I shall never fully know."

"How can you not know that side to me? I have told you about it often enough. Bless me, I am telling you about it now."

This remark made me chuckle.

"Yes, you are right," I allowed, "sometimes I do not see things clearly, even when it is before my very eyes. Sometimes I feel as if I have never known myself fully."

"Sometimes, the last things that we discover are who we truly are. It is better to ask yourself these questions now, than to ask them too late."

"Besides," I acknowledged, "you and I are similar. We do not sit and wait for things. We rise up, and we act. Perhaps, our situations are the same, only in the sense that we must look to the future. You act as you do to save your life, and I act to save my family. Therefore, since we are both women of action, I need your help."

"How?"

"Before I leave, is there any way that you can innocently discover from Miss de Bourgh, the address to Mr. Darcy's townhouse?"

"Yes, I believe that I can get an answer of that without raising suspicion."

"Thank you."

"So, what do you plan to do with this information?"

I smiled.

"Find my future. And take back my life."

When going into my room, though it was late at night, I could not rest. Therefore, lighting my candle, I sat down at my desk, took out my pen and paper, and began to write.

Dear Mr. Fitzwilliam Darcy,

Be not alarmed at the name on the front of this letter. I merely wrote that name, for it is improper for a woman to send a letter to a man when he is not family.

This is Miss Elizabeth Bennet, who writes this letter. Be not alarmed also, good sir, that this letter shall offer up a repetition of those sentiments that I addressed before you left Rosings Park, that were so disgusting to you.

Also, please forgive my writing this letter, and pray, do not cast it into the fire until after you have read it. I beg of you, pardon my indiscretion, and do not hold this impropriety against me for long. I am aware that my manner now is not above reproof, but I must explain myself, for, in this moment, I think it is better that you should know me.

We were interrupted the other day by Charlotte's return, and I had hoped to see you the next day so that we could discuss my feelings and the change of my mind and beliefs. Unfortunately, you had left —on the motive of being spared the pain of seeing me. I can understand your desire to quit Rosings with the desire of being away from me, for the sight of me must have caused you pain.

However, believe me, since we spoke, so much has occurred to change how I viewed everything. Knowledge has overturned the prejudice that I had improperly placed over so much of our acquaintance.

I spoke to Colonel Fitzwilliam, and he did verify all that you claimed Wickham had done. Therefore, I do not deny now that I was entirely deceived in Mr. Wickham's character. Both yours and the Colonel's testament have enlightened me and made me aware at how blind I have been. And to think, that I, who have prided myself on my powers of deduction, as well as who often laughed at the generous candor of my sister for when she would blindly accept the follies of others—to be now knocked down so easily under my own foolishness. Mr. Darcy, I am horribly mortified. My embarrassment humbles me now. Therefore, believe that I am aware that you were guiltless the entire time, and I placed my faith in the wrong character.

Also, my shame goes deeper than that. For you may recall that I claimed my resentment towards you began when Mr. Wickham first informed me of your dealings with him. That was, in truth, a lie.

As shameful as this is to admit, but my opinion of you had originated from when we first met at the assembly room. First, you had refused to stand up and dance with me, then I overheard your remarks about me not being handsome enough to tempt you, and rather than dismissing this as simply a terrible first impression only, I allowed it to feed my insecurity. In short—and much to the wounding of my pride—your remarks hurt my feelings. And your manner often presented you as a person who was senseless and inconsiderate to the feelings of others. I suppose that I could have forgiven your vanity if you had not wounded mine. But my vanity was wounded in that moment, and my mind afflicted. Therefore, from that moment forward, I regarded everything you did, in a prejudicial light. I wanted to see fault, so I saw it. In that practice, you and I are alike, and we both are guilty for behaving in such a way. I had no other apology to give, no other explanation to offer, but this one, that has embarrassed me even to admit.

I am human, Mr. Darcy, and therefore, I suppose that as much as I wish to believe that I am an oak, I am not always so very strong.

And lastly, to the other charge of conflict between us, which is my sister. You stand by your belief that my sister was indifferent, and here is where we are at an impasse. For I disagree with you. I know that she loves Mr. Bingley still.

What I shall concede with is that you were not presumptuous for observing that she was indifferent to him. My sister is shy. She does not always display her feelings, for fear of imposing herself onto the world or exposing herself in any way. I always admired her for this, but I now see that her serenity leaves something wanting. Jane's perfection, ironically, is therefore, also her imperfection. This revelation is now no longer lost on my mind. I see why you thought as you did. Therefore, I understand you.

I confess, however, while I understand you, it does not mean that I shall give up. I write to inform you that I shall visit you at your home when I am in town for this month. I shall call on you before one in the afternoon, for I desire your help.

You are Bingley's friend, and I wish for you to give your consent to see if Bingley and my sister are a good match for each other. I shall attempt to persuade you. Therefore, if you would be so kind as to be willing to receive me on the day that I come, which will be within this very week, then I would be ever so humble.

And if there is any doubt in your mind now to offer me this meeting, then please remember, if Jane were your sister, would you sit still and do nothing? We are both siblings to others that we love, Mr. Darcy. And in that way, we are similar in nature.

Yours etc.
Elizabeth Bennet

Closing the letter, I wrote his name on the front, and then I began to write in the top left corner:

Mr. Byron Bennet
Longbourn
Hertfordshire

I had used my father's name as the sender's address. This would shock Mr. Darcy, but I knew this was best. For women were not meant to send men letters. Under that, I wrote my uncle's address, for that was where I was staying.

Now all that I needed was for Charlotte to give me Mr. Darcy's address.

And on the very next day, she did.

CHAPTER 19

THE DREAMS OF MICE & MEN

*I*n his townhouse, Darcy was sitting at his desk, seeing to business that was waiting for him in London. At the present moment, he was writing a letter to his tenants on his estate, who had suffered a disagreement.

Sadly when he wrote, he found himself unable to concentrate. Letting his quill rest on top of his half-finished letter, Darcy closed his eyes and rubbed his temples, frustrated.

Unable to release Elizabeth Bennet from his mind, his thoughts were never far away from Hunsford Parsonage, which was the last place that he had seen her.

And to think that when going to see her, he had been on the verge of proposing marriage to her. He thought that she would have been overjoyed and flattered by his offer. Every part of himself expected this, unable to see the hubris of this certainty.

Yet, it all resulted in him not only never being able to propose at all, but being discovered to have offended her, and that she never actually liked him to begin with.

He had now been dealt a blow, and his self-assurance and confidence were greatly affected. He felt uncertain about everything now.

For all that time, he thought that they had been getting along splendidly, that she understood him, and that her lively mind was being playful with him. But, all the while, he mistook her incivility and disdain for him for her being in love with him as well! This was overwhelming because he could not help but wonder if he had been, in some way, projecting his own desires onto her.

He was in love with her; therefore, she must naturally be in love with him.

Therefore, in all that time, was he really seeing her for what she was? Or was he seeing what he wanted to see?

"I was blinded by pride," he whispered to himself, "so terribly blinded. Nothing looks clear, as of now."

Opening his eyes, he looked down at his paper.

"I am Mr. Darcy, and I shall recover from this. I shall!"

Taking up his pen again, Mr. Darcy continued to attend to his business when his clerk entered.

"Mr. Darcy, sir," his clerk, Wilson, said. Darcy turned to him and saw that Wilson had some letters for him. "Letters arrived for you."

"Thank you," Darcy stated automatically and not attentive, "proceed as usual. State the names of the senders and organize them into two distinct piles of important versus unimportant."

"Yes, sir. First are clearly two dinner party invitations from the Coles and the Slicksons. The next is a letter from Miss Darcy and another from Mrs. Reynolds. Oh, and this last one is strange. For I have never heard someone send you a letter of this name. This is from a Mr. Byron Bennet, from Longbourn."

This perked Darcy's interest, and he looked up, alarmed.

"That cannot be correct," Darcy augmented.

"His name is written here."

"That is not possible. Mr. Byron Bennet is dead."

"Well, forgive me for sounding morbid, sir, but you have to ask yourself, why is a dead man sending you letters?"

Mr. Darcy took the letter and stared at him.

It was Elizabeth's father, the late Mr. Bennet, who had sent him a letter. Either it was a letter that was sent too late or darker forces were at work. Darcy was not the suspicious kind, so he immediately assumed that something else was going on here.

"Thank you, Wilson," Darcy responded, "sort the others into the piles while I read this one."

"Very good, sir."

Wilson sat at a desk that was on the other side of the room while Darcy opened up the letter.

"A dead man is sending me letters," he whispered to himself, "how can I resist?"

And then he began to read it…and it was no dead man at all.

CHAPTER 20

AN UNWELCOME PROPOSAL

The day of our departure from Rosings Park came, but we would be one short. Charlotte's items and belongings were relocated to Rosings, and we would depart without her.

Happy was Sir William to have one daughter so advantageously placed and in so great a home. If she would not be married, then this would easily be the next best thing.

Charlotte had been as good as her word and had gotten me Mr. Darcy's address.

"Leave the letter with me," Charlotte had whispered, "and I promise that I will be able to have it sent with the rest of Lady Catherine's mail today."

Thanking her, I had given her the letter and was glad that it would be dispatched soon. With any luck, it would arrive in London even before I did.

The farewells had been quite sincere on both sides.

Sir William and Maria had been overjoyed at coming and showed sadness at parting from Charlotte.

She and I had embraced.

Lady Catherine had informed Charlotte to tell her that she said farewell, and Anne de Bourgh probably did not care less about us.

We had entered our carriage and were off to London. As we had departed, I saw Charlotte get smaller and smaller as we drove away from her.

I had wondered if she would be happy with the life that she had now chosen, for Anne de Bourgh was such a lifeless creature, but Charlotte had walked into it with both eyes open. And if there was one chief talent that she had it was in making a new life for herself.

If the purpose of this work would be to describe the landscape that we saw on our way to town, then I would write it in detail, yet, I lack the skill. Also, Sir William, Maria and I had little to speak of that we had not already spoken of many times before.

Within half a day's time, we had arrived in Cheapside, at my Uncle Gardiner's home, where they were already expecting us.

My aunt and uncle were truly happy that we had arrived safely, and their children were all eager to see us as well. As always, when seeing my aunt and uncle in Cheapside, I was always content and overjoyed to see them.

Although, my chief concern was in seeing Jane, and when she met us, along with the rest of the family, I was happy to see that her beauty was still as luminous as ever. However, I could tell, secretly, that she perhaps was low in spirits. Despite this, she did her best to conceal it, and she did so with great fortitude.

"So," Aunt Gardiner said as we all sat down in the sitting room, "Charlotte has gone from a parsonage to a fine house."

"Happy thought indeed," Uncle Gardiner added.

"It was the most splendid thing!" Maria laughed. "And though it was a lengthy visit, it seemed as if it had only been a day or two that we were there. So much had happened!"

"Yes, indeed," Sir William said, "we were quite beside ourselves with the luxuries that we saw and the generosity that we had faced. Mr. Collins was accurate in the grandeur of Rosings Park. Though Charlotte has lost her husband in so early a time, at least she has gained the favor of a great lady. So, Rosings still has much to offer. It reminds me greatly of the day that I received my knighthood at St. James's Court."

Sir William then thought it proper to once more regale us with stories of the day that he was knighted.

When doing so, Aunt and Uncle Gardiner gave me a look, suppressed a smile, and allowed him to continue.

Sir William and Maria did not remain in London for even the entire day. He merely stopped off to deliver me safely into my relative's home, for which I was to stay for a fortnight. He was to break his journey there for an hour, and then take his chaise and four back to Hertfordshire since he had been away from home for long enough.

The Gardiners, Jane, and I offered them our farewells and were happy to still be in London.

As my luggage was being placed in the guest room, my aunt had a message for me.

"Lizzy, your presence was actually sought after here in town," she reported.

"My presence?" I asked, wondering if she was referring to Mr. Darcy or Colonel Fitzwilliam. "Someone has inquired after me?"

"Yes, for but two days ago, we received a visitor here."

"Are you going to leave me in suspense?" I asked, grinning.

"Not at all. Mr. Wickham paid us a visit the other day. And he inquired after you."

In hearing the name, my smile dropped, and my spirits along with it.

"Wickham?" I repeated. "What brought him here?"

"He came because he was hoping that perhaps you had come to visit us. Therefore, he came to see you. But, never fear, for we informed him that he was in luck. We made him aware that you would be arriving today."

"Oh," I said, not happy.

"This news seems not to be to your pleasure."

"It is… what it is. I shall say no more than that for now."

"In truth," my aunt lowered her voice and whispered, "your lack of joy in hearing this news makes me glad. You know that I find him to be a pleasant sort of man, but I never desired you to become attached to him. Lizzy, please do not tell me that you have given your heart to him."

"Aunt, I can assure you that my heart is the last thing that I shall ever give him."

My aunt smiled at this.

"I am happy we are of one mind. He is a lovely man, but it is not a prudent match."

"I have grown wiser since we last saw each other."

I went up the steps and knocked on Jane's door.

"Jane," I began, "I am ever so glad to see you looking well."

"You did not think I would let my present heartache prevent me from keeping my spirits up?" Jane smiled serenely, "I would not let myself suffer needlessly, I can assure you."

"But I know that you are not happy, Jane. I can see it in your eyes."

Jane crossed her hands and looked down at her lap.

"Is it that obvious?"

"You conceal it well, but you and I have been sisters for my entire life. You must give me credit where it is due and assume that I know you well."

"Yes, well… Lizzy, I suppose that, despite my best efforts to forget Mr. Bingley, I do still long to see him. I feel foolish for clinging to emotions that do me no good. And I am interested in your travels, I am."

"You are not being selfish by talking about your feelings. We spoke all about Kent this afternoon, and this is the evening. Talks in a bedroom are meant for topics such as this. Therefore, I am listening."

"But there is no point in me speaking about this."

"What is important to talk about is never unwise to say."

"But it is unwise. It is unwise to feel for a man who does not feel for you. Mr. Bingley does not care for me, therefore, I ought to release him from my mind."

"No, Jane. He does love you, and he is right to be in your mind still."

"You are just saying that to comfort me."

"No, I am saying it because I know it. Just like I know the

reason he has not come to you is because he is completely ignorant of you being in town. He does not even know you are here."

"What?" she asked, her eyes widening.

"Bingley is still in love with you. I know this because I was told that he was."

"By who?"

"Mr. Darcy. And now, I have much to tell you."

After I finished telling her that Darcy acknowledged to me that Bingley was never told that she was there, as well as that Bingley was convinced that she did not love him, Jane was surprised.

"His sisters convinced him to keep away from me?" She whispered, her lip trembling.

"Yes," I confirmed.

"Then perhaps it is best that I do release him, for if I cause so much disruption in their family, it would be unwise."

"You think that you ought to give Bingley up because his sisters want him to marry another woman? Is that sound? Jane, be honest with yourself. Do you really feel inclined to give up a man that you love just because his sisters want him to make an advantageous match?"

"You know very well that I could not give him up for anything."

"Then, do not give him up."

"But how shall I see him again? What am I to do? How am I to begin?"

"I have a plan. Give me time to form and shape it. If I am successful, then I will tell you what we ought to do next."

"Lizzy, it will not get you into any trouble, will it?"

"Not a jot," I lied, smiling.

"I always was a little envious at your ability to act on your own impulses."

"And I always envied your serene nature. There now, we each were jealous of each other!"

We both chuckled at this.

"I missed you," Jane said.

"You better have."

The next day, I felt as if I had not a moment to lose! I had not even the desire to wait for a couple of days but thought it wise to act now, before I lost my nerve.

Down the street from my uncle's home was his factory. Next to it were some stables. I easily could go down there and pay one of the stable hands to drive me to Grosvenor Square, where Mr. Darcy lived.

It was a plan that would be perfect and easy to achieve. Therefore, once we had breakfast and I could excuse myself, claiming that I just wished to take a brief walk around the street, I would set out on my own and seek out Mr. Darcy's home. I was taking a risk—a large one. For if Mr. Darcy disregarded it, then I would stand there, knocking on a door that would not be answered.

However, I was determined, and that was that!

After breakfast was done, I prepared myself for my grand adventure, when the bell had wrung, and we had a visitor.

Assuming this was simply one of Uncle Gardiner's business associates, I got on my coat and prepared myself to leave, when the door opened, and I froze in place.

"Miss Elizabeth!" Mr. Wickham said, bowing as he saw me from the doorway.

Mr. Wickham had called again at Cheapside.

Mr. Wickham was before me!

This was the first time that I had seen him since learning his true nature from Mr. Darcy and the Colonel.

"Mr. Wickham!" I gasped, and I felt my face blush.

"I can see that my arrival surprises you," he grinned, entering, "I flatter that it is not an unwelcome surprise."

"No," I blurted out without thinking. "No, I merely did not expect to see you, sir."

"Were you not informed that I had called before?"

"Yes, and I was surprised to hear of that as well."

"My regiment has come to town for the training grounds, and therefore, we shall be here briefly. I could not help but take advantage of this opportunity of coming to call on you."

We were interrupted by my aunt, who had entered and invited

Wickham into the sitting room. Jane and the Gardiner children came in as well, sat down, and the usual inquiries were made.

The Gardiners had a small yard behind their home, which Aunt Gardiner had turned into a small, but pretty garden. Wickham requested that he would like to take a turn in it, and requested my company to join him.

I looked around at everyone, but after a second's hesitation, I accepted.

We got our coats on and went outside. The garden was small, but it offered the chief thing that I knew Wickham had desired: intimacy.

"You are looking very well, Miss Elizabeth," Wickham said.

"Thank you," I sighed out, "and you are wearing your regimentals. Therefore, you look distinguished."

"Thank you." After a moment's silence, he continued to speak, "Miss Elizabeth, forgive me, but we have often been open with each other. Therefore, I wish to believe that I am not giving offense when I choose to notice that there is a distance between us now. Am I correct in presuming that this silence comes because you have heard of my history with Miss King?"

"Is it true? Did you really break off the engagement with her?"

"Yes, I did."

I half-believed him. At this point, he had lied so often that I still was doubtful about this report being true.

"I was surprised by this," I voiced, trying to avoid being silent. "For, I was certain that you had resolved on marrying to achieve your fortune."

"I was. And then I discovered something else."

"And what was that?"

"I discovered that maybe I could find a way to earn a living. That maybe I could find my wealth by my own merit, and that there was such a woman who would be willing to marry me, despite that I do not bring a fortune to the match. And that we would simply have to learn to economize."

"But can you, sir?" I asked. "Can you see yourself being the sort to survive off of a modest income?"

"I thought that I could not, but perhaps the demands of my

heart are more vital than the demands of my pocketbook. Miss Bennet—dearest, loveliest Elizabeth! Since the moment of our acquaintance, I have come to develop an attachment towards you that, at first, I dismissed as a passing folly. Yet now, as time has continued on, you are the first sort of woman who I could fancy seeing myself spend the rest of my life with."

Hearing these words astonished me! I felt my body grow cold, my heart freeze over, and my body stiffen. For truly, what was happening?

"Therefore," Mr. Wickham continued, getting down on one knee, "I was wondering if you would consider me? Miss Elizabeth, I offer you my hand in marriage. What say you? Will you marry me, my dear friend? Will you be my wife and make me the happiest of men?"

Mr. Wickham was proposing to me...

All the world felt as if it was in confusion, and reality appeared to be upside down as a whirlwind filled my mind.

End of Book I

Don't miss out on your next favorite book!

Join the Satin Romance mailing list
www.satinromance.com/mail.html

Coming in 2021
Chances Come, Chances Series, Book 2

Also coming in 2021
Flaws & Felicity: Pride & Prejudice
Told from the eyes of Jane Bennet. Book 1 of a new trilogy.

THANK YOU FOR READING

Did you enjoy this book?

We invite you to leave a review at your favorite book site, such as Goodreads, Amazon, Barnes & Noble, etc.

DID YOU KNOW THAT LEAVING A REVIEW…

- Helps other readers find books they may enjoy.
- Gives you a chance to let your voice be heard.
- Gives authors recognition for their hard work.
- Doesn't have to be long. A sentence or two about why you liked the book will do.

ABOUT THE AUTHOR

Ney Mitch has been a long-standing Jane Austen enthusiast, having written forty novels that were inspired by her various works. Since stumbling on Miss Austen's books after graduating from college, she has always dabbled in Austen inspired literature, ranging from writing works for teens to adults. Originally, her desire was to adapt Jane Austen's writing in a way to help young adults connect with her, however over time, she has spread her aims to other genres and styles. Having received her BA Degree at Desales University, she is a writer, both literary and dramatic, as well as being a Historic Reenactor.

facebook.com/courtney.mitchell.589

twitter.com/CMMitchelPsyche

pinterest.com/shebaanna